THE THRIFTY WITCH'S BOOK OF SIMPLE SPELLS

Inspiring | Educating | Creating | Entertaining

Brimming with creative inspiration, how-to projects, and useful information to enrich your everyday life, Quarto Knows is a favorite destination for those pursuing their interests and passions. Visit our site and dig deeper with our books into your area of interest: Quarto Creates, Quarto Cooks, Quarto Homes, Quarto Lives, Quarto Drives, Quarto Explores, Quarto Gifts, or Quarto Kids.

First Published in 2021 by Fair Winds Press, an imprint of The Quarto Group,
100 Cummings Center, Suite 265-D, Beverly, MA 01915, USA.
T (978) 282-9590 F (978) 283-2742 QuartoKnows.com

Fair Winds Press titles are also available at discount for retail, wholesale, promotional, and bulk purchase. For details, contact the Special Sales Manager by email at specialsales@quarto.com or by mail at The Quarto Group, Attn: Special Sales Manager, 100 Cummings Center, Suite 265-D, Beverly, MA 01915, USA.

26 25 24 23 22   1 2 3 4 5

ISBN: 978-1-59233-980-8

Digital edition published in 2022
eISBN: 978-1-63159-939-2

Library of Congress Cataloging-in-Publication Data

Names: Maple, Wren, author.
Title: The thrifty witch's book of simple spells : potions, charms, and
   incantations for the modern witch / Wren Maple.
Description: Beverly, MA : Fair Winds Press, 2021. | Includes index.
Identifiers: LCCN 2021029411 (print) | LCCN 2021029412 (ebook) | ISBN
   9781592339808 | ISBN xxxxxxxxxxxxx (eISBN)
Subjects: LCSH: Witchcraft. | Incantations. | Charms. | Magic.
Classification: LCC BF1566 .M2925 2021 (print) | LCC BF1566 (ebook) | DDC
   133.4/3--dc23
LC record available at https://lccn.loc.gov/2021029411
LC ebook record available at https://lccn.loc.gov/2021029412

Design, page layout, and illustration: Tanya Jacobson, jcbsn.co

Printed in China

The information in this book is for educational purposes only. It is not intended to replace the advice of a physician or medical practitioner. Please see your health-care provider before beginning any new health program.

THE Thrifty Witch's BOOK OF SIMPLE Spells

WREN MAPLE

POTIONS, CHARMS, AND INCANTATIONS FOR THE MODERN WITCH

FAIR WINDS

Contents

Introduction

LIKE MANY THINGS, WITCHCRAFT IS WHAT YOU MAKE IT.

For me, witchcraft is a practice in self-care and spirituality. It is a way for me to assert control in an uncontrolled environment. It is a path forward, a means to an existence characterized by reward.

I cast spells for my best life. I cast what I need to or what the moment calls for in order for me to feel good and live well.

I've cast spells with a coven and alone in the dark at 3 a.m. I cast healing spells for loved ones. I cast confidence spells, love spells, protection spells, psychic spells, banishing and binding spells, chakra spells, sleep spells, and so many, many more spells that I'm sure I can't recall no matter how long I sit here.

In short, witchcraft is the manifestation of how I picture my greatest life.

THRIFTINESS

Thrifty witchcraft means something different for everyone.

Some witches may exclusively use whatever is already in their home or garden for spells, while others feel comfortable setting a budget for materials relative to their income.

Whatever you decide, my goal for these spell is to keep the ingredients easy to find and fairly low cost.

And while I want to keep my spells interesting by not using the same materials over and over again, you'll find that many do, in fact, cross over.

There are other ways to stay thrifty in your craft: You needn't use an entire candle for one spell, and if you don't have one of the materials, you can skip it.

Plus, clear quartz is the universal substitute, so if you aren't willing to spend money on a stone, just stick with the master healer.

Witchcraft knows no age, gender, or sex. The general public tends to associate witchcraft with adult women, but I know plenty of male and nonbinary witches.

Witchcraft itself is not a religion; it may or may not be a facet *of* a religion such as Wicca. It is an ancient spiritual practice; it was here long before Christianity came about. It has origins in countless cultures and traditions. Unlike many religions, witchcraft is personal and customizable to the witch.

In a sense, it's hedonism; we witches follow our hearts and cast spells to get what we want. It does not follow the guise of most religions in that the participants must sacrifice their desires to fit the moral bill of some higher power.

Despite what many of my followers believe, I am not a Wiccan. In fact, I don't subscribe to any religion. You don't need to, to practice witchcraft.

Meanwhile, ethics within witchcraft vary. Wiccans, for example, believe in the Rule of Three—whatever is put out in the world will return threefold. Wiccans believe in the karmic effects of spells.

I simply follow what feels right; something I've dubbed my "witchy intuition."

Before we go any further, let me just say: Witchcraft is, on the whole, *not* like the movies. Your favorite pop media witches are fun, but don't let Hollywood's imagination interfere with how you practice. Definitely don't buy into the negative portrayals out there: Witchcraft is neither shameful nor evil. Actually, if done properly, witchcraft heals and uplifts.

Along those same lines, unlike in the movies, there are no mistakes in witchcraft. And though you may feel like an imposter sometimes—I know I do!—this feeling doesn't detract from your innate power. When you get in a rut or doubt your abilities, remember that witchcraft is a learned skill. Forgive yourself. Take all the time you need to get back on the horse. When you do, this book will be here to help guide you.

There is no right or wrong way to cast a spell. There is no right way or wrong way to be a witch. There are no requirements to witchcraft; if you're reading this book, you are inherently witchy.

You may simply call yourself a witch. In fact, there is great power in announcing it.

You may practice once a week; you may practice once a month. I like to practice at least once weekly, because I believe the more often I cast, the better I become at witchcraft as a whole. The greater the frequency at which I cast, the greater the success rate of my spells; *practice makes perfect* applies just as well to witchcraft as any other craft.

And so, no need to dwell on this or that, what you need, what you don't have—use what you do have, and just *cast*. If you don't have any ingredients, you may simply walk beneath the light of the moon and pray. Remember, a witch's most valuable possession is their intention.

You already have what you need. So, let's get started!

ch.1

GETTING STARTED

Witchcraft is 90 percent intention and 10 percent using tools in a ritual way. Those tools may include candles, cauldrons, food items, herbs, salt and pepper, stones, twine, water, and more. We'll explore these materials and their purposes in this chapter. But first, let's look at the types of witchcraft and what witches do.

Types of Witches

What type of witch are you? Knowing the answer to this question is not just about the religious and symbolic elements of witchcraft you are drawn to. Identifying the type of witch you are can also help you decide what practices and tools you want to explore, and it can help you connect with—and grow with—your community. Here are some of the types of witches you may encounter.

- **Eclectic witch:** An eclectic witch draws inspiration from a variety of practices. I'm an eclectic witch because I don't subscribe to any single genre of witchcraft. As an agnostic, I tend to pray to the universe as a divine entity, leaving room for whatever may be. When I call on deities, it is as a form of symbolism. I also pray to my dad, who passed away in 2019. Communing with the dead is not my specialty, but it feels nice to call on him in spells. Eclectic witches pray to whomever they choose, and they mix various elements of differing practices. An eclectic witch may not subscribe to the Wiccan Rede, for example, but may celebrate the Wheel of the Year (Wiccan holidays).

- **Elemental witch:** An elemental witch casts a circle before spells and works heavily with the elements—water, fire, air, Earth, and Spirit (the fifth element).

- **Folk/traditional witch:** Folk or traditional witches practice in alignment with their heritage or the deep traditions entrenched in the culture of their geographical area. For example, my lineage is mainly Celtic, so I've begun to look into Celtic practices within witchcraft. I tend to associate the fold or traditional witch with Appalachian witchcraft.

- **Hedge/hearth witch:** A hedge witch, or hearth witch, considers the hearth and home to be the epicenter for spellcraft. These witches typically cast alone, and they value herbs and their magickal associations.

- **Kitchen witch:** A kitchen witch infuses food with intention by using a blend of cooking and spellcasting. For example, a kitchen witch may infuse her dinner with dill and the intention to attract money.

Deities

Deities, or gods and goddesses, are revered by some witches. For others, they serve as symbols, represented through various spellwork. Secular witches choose not to work with deities. You may feel the call to worship, pray to, or work with a deity—for example, by calling on them to help you with a spell or designating space for them on your altar. It's totally up to you and your practice!

Witches tend to worship various deities. You can do more research into or work with a deity you feel drawn to. Some of the most popular deities are:

- **Aphrodite:** Greek goddess of love and beauty
- **Athena:** Greek goddess of wisdom and war
- **Brighid:** Celtic goddess of art and healing
- **Frigg:** Norse goddess of marriage and the hearth
- **Gaia:** Greek goddess of Earth
- **Hecate:** Greek goddess of witchcraft
- **Isis:** Egyptian mother goddess of nature

- **Luna:** Roman goddess of the moon
- **Ma'at:** Egyptian goddess of truth and justice
- **Oshun:** Yoruban river goddess
- **Rhiannon:** Celtic goddess of the moon
- **Selene:** Greek goddess of the moon
- **Sophia:** Greek goddess of wisdom
- **Yemeya:** Yoruban mother goddess

FINDING YOUR OWN WAY

Don't be overwhelmed by the amount of information you might encounter as you begin your witchcraft journey. There's no need to memorize anything. I frequently research all facets of the craft, and I only remember certain things because of continuous practice.

Also, social media sometimes gets a bad rap, but it can serve as a wonderful tool within modern witchcraft. It's a great place for beginners to learn, ask questions, and get involved in the community. Some witches like to post on social media about the spells they cast, and it can serve as inspiration for those just starting out, as well as for more advanced witches.

Witchcraft is ultimately about intention, so don't worry if you're not sure that something you read online is 100 percent accurate. Spirituality doesn't rely on facts in the end. There's no one true source of witchcraft. One herb can serve multiple purposes to multiple witches.

Do be careful not to step on other cultures in your practice. I tend to stay away from certain herbs due to appropriation, overharvesting, and the trampling of cultures that are historically oppressed.

This may sound cheesy, but it's important that you have fun. Witchcraft should not feel stressful, religious (unless you'd like it to be), demanding, or emotionally taxing. In fact, it should feel quite the opposite! For me, witchcraft serves as a reprieve from the stressors of daily life. It's where I can gather my intention for my life and focus on what *I* need. It's meditative—I typically finish spells feeling more relaxed. If it doesn't feel good, take a break and come back to it later (or not at all—you can always scrap a spell if it doesn't feel right).

If you happen to falter during a spell (performing a step out of order, mispronouncing something, etc.), don't worry. It's not like in *Harry Potter*—real-life witchcraft doesn't work like that. In fact, if you mess up, there's really no need to start over. Just roll with it, unless you can't let it go.

Don't push or overexert yourself. Do what feels right, when it feels right.

Divination

The bulk of witchcraft comprises casting spells and divination. Divination means interpreting, understanding, or relaying a message from a higher power to you or whomever you're divining for. There are several common methods of divination, including the following:

- **Automatic writing:** Automatic writing involves entering a meditative state and writing in a stream of consciousness.

- **Bibliomancy:** Bibliomancy is the use of writing in a sacred book (or just a book that's special to you) to receive a message.

- **Oracle cards:** Think of oracle cards somewhat like fortune cookies: they may not be as detailed as tarot cards, but they can give you a glance at a big picture.

- **Pendulum:** A pendulum (typically a stone) can be used to answer yes/no/maybe questions.

- **Runes:** Reading runes involves throwing stones with sacred symbols on them to receive a message.

- **Scrying:** Staring into a surface, such as a crystal, fire, or water, until you see a message or image is called scrying. Wax scrying is a little different; it consists of pouring wax into a bowl of water and making sense of the images.

- **Tarot:** Tarot card spreads or pulls can be used to divine. Tarot decks consist of major arcana and minor arcana cards. They are not to be confused with oracle cards.

Divining, like spellcraft, is a learned skill. It's a little more difficult, however, because you're not simply following a set of instructions. Not all witches divine, and that's okay. You may find yourself pulled to a form of divination at some point in your witchy journey. If you feel this pull, I encourage you to act on it. Do research, gather the necessary tools, and try your hand. Don't worry if you don't get a clear read right away. It takes practice.

Whatever form of divination calls to you, pick just one and practice daily. The message isn't always clear, and at times, you'll doubt your prowess. Remember: Divination is a learned skill for those enticed by the occult; you already possess the interest! Push through the uncertainty and continue your studies. Exercise your abilities solo, then work your way up to divining for friends and family.

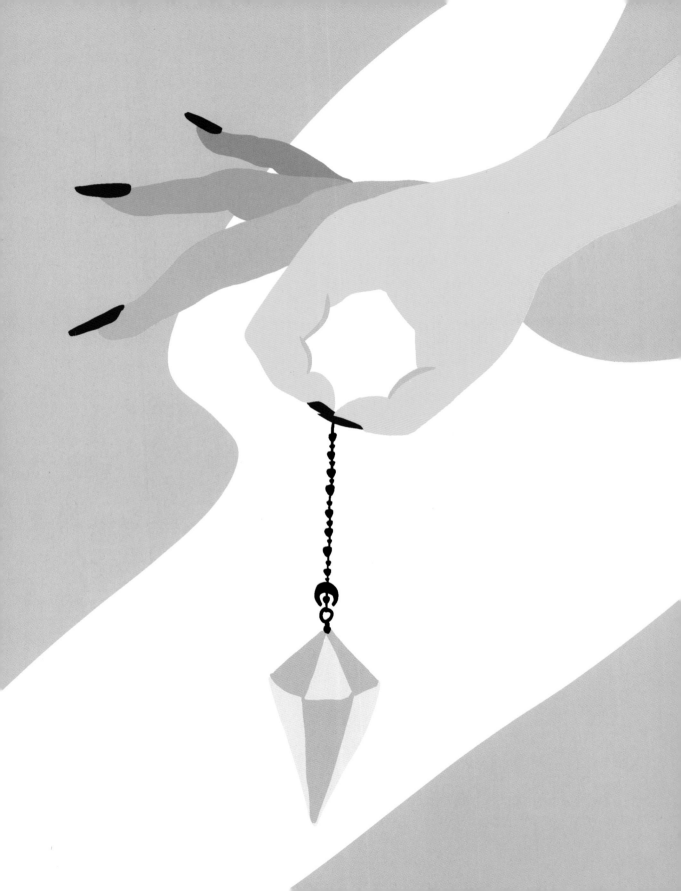

A Witch's Guide to Herbs

Herbs are some of the most effective—and most readily available—tools in a new witch's collection. You may already have many of these herbs in your kitchen! Here are some to consider stocking up on, along with their magickal uses and associations. If you can't find a particular herb locally, you're sure to find it online. Etsy is a good place to find the more niche herbs, and it's a great opportunity to support small businesses. However, herbs aren't required for any spell; they're just nice to have! Don't feel like you have to buy every herb listed here. Either fresh or dried herbs can be used for the spells throughout this book, but fresh ingredients will need to be replaced fairly quickly.

Anise Use anise to promote happiness, stave off the evil eye, and stimulate intuition. Sprinkle anise in jar spells for psychic wisdom. Keep near your pillow to prevent nightmares. Hang anise in a pouch around your bed to restore youthfulness and vitality.

Basil This herb can attract money, romance, sympathy, prosperity, and general success. You can use it in protection or deflection spells to dispel unwanted negativity.

Bay Leaf Use bay leaves for protection and strength or to purify an area or object, bring about good luck, and foster psychic wisdom.

Bay Leaf

Basil

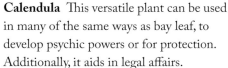

Calendula This versatile plant can be used in many of the same ways as bay leaf, to develop psychic powers or for protection. Additionally, it aids in legal affairs.

Cardamom This herb can be used in spells pertaining to love, romance, and sensuality.

Calendula

Cardamom

Chamomile

Chamomile You may already be a drinker of chamomile tea as it is widely known for its properties of relaxation. Its magickal uses move in the same way; it can be used in spells to decrease stress or other meditative purposes. However, it can also be used in spells that will ultimately increase your sense of well-being and relaxation—for example, building wealth or finding love.

Clove A highly protective spice, clove prevents negativity from entering a space, attracts wealth, dispels hostility, and brings about clarity.

Coriander

Dill

Eucalyptus

Coriander There are many ways to use coriander; its special uses include enhancing love (by adding seeds to a pouch or jar spell), improving health, and providing protection. Instill a sense of peace in your home by tying coriander with white ribbon and hanging it in the entryways and living spaces.

Dill While it's easy to think of pickles at first when adding dill to a spell, this herb is one you can use in the bath or shower to help attract love! You can also use it in spells to increase your wealth and promote good luck.

Eucalyptus Eucalyptus is not only good for keeping your bathroom smelling nice; it also aids in purification, healing, protection, and relationship matters.

Fennel seeds Great for protection jars or pouch spells, fennel seeds protect, cleanse, heal, and strengthen. Sprinkle fennel seeds in your windows and doors to guard against negativity.

Garlic This eliminates negativity, wards off vampires (if you believe in them), purifies objects, cleanses spaces, and safeguards against psychic attacks and malevolent spirits.

Ginger Increase the strength of any spellwork by using ginger. This draw in love, lust, romantic and general energy, spontaneity, and adventure. It may also improve health.

Juniper Juniper helps you manifest good health, money, and love. Burn for protection and joy. Toss juniper berries in spell jars or pouches for romance. Use juniper oil to attract wealth and prosperity. Keep sprigs of juniper with your valuables to fend off theft.

Lavender Lavender is a soothing herb frequently relied on to reduce stress and anxiety. It promotes love, health, and well-being. It's also helpful to some for more restful sleep.

Juniper

Lavender

Lemon Balm

Lemon balm This is used in spells for healing, attracting your soulmate, spiritual aid, intuition, and meeting goals.

Magnolia flowers These flowers promote peace in relationships, calm nerves, enhance health and beauty, increase love and loyalty, and may help one rise above addictions and obsessions.

Milk thistle Milk thistle brings about resilience and strength and assists in making difficult decisions by imparting wisdom.

Oregano Oregano is used for endurance; perseverance in life matters; and increased energy, youthfulness, and enthusiasm.

Magnolia Flower

Oregeno

Parsley Parsley helps generate wealth and prosperity, provides good luck, and fosters a sense of tranquility and well-being. This herb promotes lust, purity and health and may enhance strength after surgery.

Peppermint Peppermint will help raise the vibrations of a space, bring about sound sleep and psychic dreams, and facilitate change in one's life. Use for money magick and to encourage healing. Peppermint purifies and clears stagnant energy.

Rosemary Wash your hands with water and rosemary before performing healing spells. It promotes restful sleep. Burn to purify a space and banish negative energy. An all-purpose herb often used as a substitute for others, rosemary may help improve memory, assist in academic studies, and draw in lust and love.

Sage Sage purifies and banishes negativity, stimulates mental strength, may heal a space or person, and draws in psychic wisdom. It protects against grief and loss.

Tarragon Tarragon inspires compassion, bravery, protection, and harmony.

Thyme Thyme's magickal properties include banishment and purification, bravery and strength, and wealth and prosperity. It can increase the loyalty and affection of a loved one. Wear a sprig on your person to defend against grief. Hang in your home to cleanse the space. Place near your pillow to keep nightmares at bay.

Yarrow flower This plant attracts romance, healing, confidence, and psychic wisdom. It assists in conquering fears. Gift newlyweds a jar of yarrow flower, thyme, magnolia flowers, juniper berries, and rose quartz for happiness and stability in their marriage.

Parsley

Peppermint

Rosemary

Sage

Tarragon

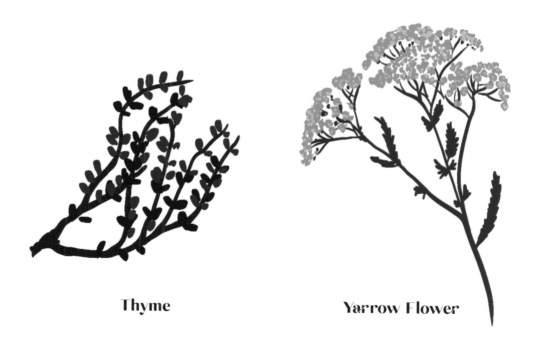

Thyme

Yarrow Flower

A Witch's Guide to Stones

Many witches enjoy working with crystals, minerals, and other stones. Some believe stones contain magickal properties or are associated with magick. To that end, certain stones will align with your spellcraft. For example, citrine is great to work with when you need a creative boost or a dose of happiness, and amethyst is wonderful for psychic spellwork and anything dealing with anxiety or stress. Clear quartz is probably the most popular crystal to work with, as it's highly accessible and can be programmed with any intention you like. There are hundreds of stones; if you'd like to learn about the unique properties of each, I recommend *The Crystal Bible* by Judy Hall. I've referenced her work a lot in my studies and spellwork.

Note: Water-safe stones are any from the quartz family (amethyst, citrine, clear quartz, smoky quartz). Otherwise, keep crystals out of and away from water to prevent damaging them!

Cleansing Crystals

You can use smoke cleansing for any crystal. Buy a bundle of the herb you want to use for cleansing, such as bay leaf, juniper, lemongrass, mugwort, pine, or rosemary, being mindful of how the herb was grown and that it is not overharvested. Just follow your intention and what you feel drawn to. Light the herb bundle, then hold the stone in its smoke. I like to turn the stone in the smoke to make sure every angle is saturated. You can do a meditation, if you want. Envision the stagnant and old energy lifting from the stone. Close your eyes and repeat a mantra, or simply say the word *cleanse*.

Another way to cleanse a crystal is with an essential oil elixir spray. Mist it into the air and pass the stone through the droplets. You can do this with just about any stone, as long as you spray the elixir in the air and not directly on the stone. Use a similar visualization exercise as when using smoke to cleanse.

The easiest way to cleanse stones is simply to put them in a bowl with the crystal selenite, or use a bowl made from selenite. You can still do the visual exercise or mantra, but leave the stones overnight to cleanse. If the timing is right, do this same thing with the full moon. Place your crystals on a window ledge or outside (in nice weather) and make sure the full moon's light hits them. Light a candle and visualize as you would with other cleansing methods. Make sure to thank the moon and include gratitude as part of the process.

WITCHY TIP: TALK TO YOUR CRYSTALS

After cleansing your crystals, talk to them about what you want. You may feel silly, but there are a couple benefits to this:

1 You're speaking your intentions aloud, bringing them into focus and progressing the process of manifestation.

2 You're programming your stones with aspirations, strengthening their properties, and enhancing their power overall.

Here are the crystals used or suggested for use in this book:

- Amethyst
- Angelite
- Apache tears
- Apatite
- Black kyanite
- Black tourmaline
- Bloodstone
- Blue chalcedony
- Carnelian
- Chrysocolla
- Citrine
- Clear quartz
- Desert rose selenite
- Fire agate

- Fluorite
- Garnet
- Golden rutilated quartz
- Green aventurine
- Hematite
- Kunzite
- Labradorite
- Lapis lazuli
- Larimar
- Lepidolite
- Malachite
- Moonstone
- Moss agate
- Obsidian

- Pyrite
- Rainbow fluorite
- Red jasper
- Rhodochrosite
- Rhodonite
- Rose quartz
- Ruby
- Selenite
- Smoky quartz
- Sodalite
- Tiger's eye
- Turquoise
- Yellow calcite

WITCHY TIP: FORGE A BOND WITH A CRYSTAL

Pick a crystal for today. Hold it in your hand like you would a delicate creature. Whisper your intentions to it; carry it on your person until the day's end. (You may even sleep with it tonight, if you wish.)

Other Magickal Tools and Techniques

The rest of the contents of your witchy toolbox will depend on what sort of spellcraft and divination you're drawn to or you want to try. Here are some things you might want to have on hand:

- **Bathtub:** If there's no place in your house to get privacy for a spell, consider the bathtub. Even if you have a dedicated spell area, the bathtub can be a powerful change of scenery. It allows you to incorporate the element of water into your spellwork. The bath will also relax you. Turn out the lights, light some candles, bring some quartz stones into the bath with you—create a powerful spell space.
- **Candles:** Spell candles are typically 4 inches (10 cm) long. You can get them affordably on Etsy or Amazon. I like to pick my candle color based on the intention of my spell (more on color meanings following). You can pray over your candle, chant over your candle, or the like. I like to set up my stones around my candles to make a mini shrine. I also use candles when I'm taking a bath because 1) it's relaxing; 2) you're combining the water and fire elements; and 3) I think it lends extra power to the experience.

You can let your candle burn down all the way during every spell (lots of witches do this), or you can blow out the candle and make a wish, like a birthday candle. Speaking of which, birthday candles are available at the dollar store and can totally be used for spellwork! Some witches, however, don't believe in blowing out the candle because they think it's disrespectful to the fire element, so they snuff it. It's up to you and your practice.

- **Cauldron:** I believe every witch should have a cast-iron cauldron, unless they have a fireplace. It's a safe and portable place to burn things. Cauldrons also last a long time and, thus, are a worthwhile investment.
- **Coffee:** To bring energy to your spells.
- **Essential oils:** I find oils useful but expensive. Invest in those that are the most useful to the spells you want to cast. I use rosemary essential oil like I use clear quartz—it's great in so many situations. Basil, frankincense, lemon, and ylang-ylang essential oils are among my other favorites. Lavender is great for sleep spells. If you use essential oils on your skin, dilute them first with a carrier oil (like almond or jojoba) and do a patch test to check for any negative reactions.

- **Freezer:** Put your binding spell creation (for example, a name in a lemon, see page 117) in the freezer to freeze continued action.

- **Full moon water:** Create this magickal elixir, generally including water, herbs, and stones and infused with your intentions, and leave it out on the night of the full moon.

- **Incense:** There are other uses for incense in witchcraft, but I mainly like to light it before spells to create a meditative mood. Be careful using incense around kids or pets.

- **Mugs/glasses/spoons:** These vessels are generally used for consumable spells, such as tea spells, which I'm a huge fan of—so simple and hydrating! Stir clockwise with your spoon to bring something into your life and counterclockwise to banish something from your life.

- **Pouches:** For pouch spells. Use different colors for different associations. See the list on the following page.

- **Twine:** For knot spells.

WITCHY TIP: MAGICKAL USES FOR COFFEE

- Add it to your bathwater to release negative thoughts.
- Arrange a circle of coffee beans around your stones, candles, or any spellwork to speed it up or increase its strength.
- Drink it in the morning to promote energy.
- Sip it while meditating to overcome energetic blockages.
- Sleep with coffee grounds in a sachet beneath your pillow to ward off nightmares.
- Step on old coffee grounds (or take a foot bath with old grounds) for grounding.

Color Meanings

As you gather your supplies, check the range of colors they come in—the greater the range, the better. You may want to use the color of your candles, drawing symbols, pouches, or the like to enhance certain aspects of your spellwork. Here are some color associations you can draw on:

- **Black:** Strongly dispels negative energy, banishes, cleanses, protects
- **Blue:** Meditation, calm, peace
- **Brown:** Earth-centered spells, grounding
- **Gold:** Solar energy, connecting with masculine energy, pagan gods
- **Green:** Nature, healing, money
- **Orange:** Energy, creativity, innovation
- **Purple:** Connecting with the divine/deities and psychic wisdom
- **Red:** Passion, lust, zest, ambition
- **Silver:** Lunar energy, connecting with feminine energy, pagan goddesses
- **White:** Peace, truth, purity, gently dispelling negativity
- **Yellow:** Intelligence, focus, joy

Elements

Some witches call forth the elements to cast a protective circle before a spell. I don't typically do this because I don't feel it's necessary, but you may. And if you do, you will want to include a representation of each element on your altar. Here are some examples:

- **Air:** Steam from a bath, going outside when it's windy, taking deep breaths
- **Earth:** Things you find outside such as stones, leaves, or dirt. Make sure to give back to Earth what you take from it.
- **Fire:** Candles, cauldrons, bonfires
- **Water:** Bathwater, drinking water, moon water
- **Spirit (fifth element):** Whatever deity you work with, the divine universe, spirit guides

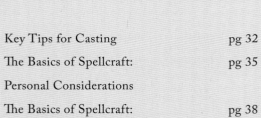

ch.2

TECHNIQUES, TIPS, AND TRICKS FOR CASTING

S o, you are ready to cast your first spell—congratulations, you made it this far! Before you begin, there are a few things to keep in mind. You'll want to meditate; set your intention; arrange your spell space; consider an herbal cleanse of your area, stones, and aura; and understand your relationship with the moon (see page 43).

That sounds like a lot! But, the most important thing to remember is, although I've included plenty of information for you, there's no reason to overthink it. After all, witchcraft isn't something you can ever perfect, per se—it's an ongoing *practice*. And while it might sound cliché, I believe witchcraft should be fun. That means it shouldn't seem like homework (so, if you ever get to the point where it does, take a break).

It's not necessary to incorporate each of my techniques to start—you can begin any time! These are just topics that may help you elevate your work, and a few ways to unstick yourself if you feel stuck before casting.

I'd say, "good luck," but I know you don't need it!

Key Tips for Casting

We'll discuss some of these topics in more depth later, but this list covers what I consider crucial for my casting.

1   **Find the right location.** Although you should seek out a quiet environment, you can cast most spells almost anywhere.

2   **Meditate, meditate, meditate.** I can't stress this enough: One of the best ways you can prepare for spellcraft is through meditation (see page 35).

3   **Don't worry about casting each step of your spells perfectly.** A perfectly cast spell is like a wedding day with zero hiccups: It typically doesn't happen. Don't worry if you laugh or feel ridiculous. Don't concern yourself if your dog starts barking or your roommate barges in mid-incantation. That's life. You don't need to start over if you mess up, unless you won't feel settled until you do so. You're not going to accidentally curse yourself or someone else if you don't get it exactly right. But because your intention and state of mind are important, take stock before moving on.

4   **Never downplay the significance of intent.** Spells are simply the application of intent informed by action through the use of natural tools. Intent itself is the most important element of spellcraft. The energy you bring to your spell will reflect the results: If you're optimistic about your work, you're far more likely to succeed (see page 37).

5   **Work with the moon to heighten your magick.** It's no secret that witches are enamored of the moon. If you'd like, time your spells by its phases (see page 43).

6   **Start most of your spellwork with a cleansing ritual.** Ritualistic cleansing through the burning of special herbs will help clear your mind's clutter and set your intentions for the forthcoming spell. Alternatively, you can use an elixir with essential oils, herbal infusions, and even crystals. I typically cleanse before spells to calm my overactive nervous system and get in the witchy zone.

What, specifically, should be cleansed before your spells? Your aura, for one—be sure to (safely) wave the smoke around your body to eliminate or unstick stagnant energy, either from yourself or from others you've encountered. Feel free to wear a mask to protect your lungs. If you use a liquid elixir, dab it on your chakras or spray the air around yourself.

I also like to cleanse my stones, so they can better work their magick. It's like gifting them a spiritual shower—you tend to feel fresher and less jumbled after a long, hot soak and the same applies to your crystals. If you're using an elixir to cleanse your stones, make sure they're water-safe!

Typically, I repeat a mantra during this time. Here are examples of mantras I use:

"Remove that which obstructs clarity."

"Suffuse the atmosphere with joy."

"Clear the air; refine for the divine."

"Purge my space of that which corrodes."

7   **The more you do it, the better you'll get.** You've probably heard that practice makes perfect. Although you may never cast a spell *flawlessly*, establishing a weekly spell ritual serves to sharpen your craft. The continuation of spellwork will enhance your results, enabling you to achieve all that you desire. It will also make you a more powerful witch. And practicing spells will show you the kind of magick you're drawn to and may help you identify your brand of witchcraft.

The Basics of Spellcraft: Personal Considerations

There are two key areas to prepare before spellcraft: environmental and personal.

Preparing the environmental aspects means, for example, working on the space in which you will be casting, selecting the right herbs and stones, and timing your spell by the moon's cycle.

But if you don't prepare your personal aspects—if you're not prepared to allow magick into your life, if you have doubts about your abilities or witchcraft, in general, or the like—your spells won't do much good. I believe that your personal preparation is the most important factor in casting.

You need to be ready to accept that the world around you perhaps isn't exactly what it seems and that there may be supernatural/divine (or otherwise beyond secular) forces at play that you may harness for your greater/higher good and for the greater/higher good of others.

The Meditative State

The meditative state may look different for each person. There are many schools of thought surrounding meditation, including transcendentalism and mindfulness, and one may work better for you than another.

What you should know is that spellcraft frequently utilizes a discipline called *focused intention*, which incorporates visualizations, incantations, or some other creative expression to manifest something in your life. Therefore, I find it helpful to meditate before performing the spell itself. I recommend getting comfortable in a meditative state before you meditate on something specific.

I find mindfulness to be the easiest form of meditation for those who are beginners (and look, most of us—myself included—are beginners!). Mindfulness is all about staying present and observing what's passing through and around you rather than working to clear your mind. It's a difficult task, if you ask me! But luckily, you don't need to be a guru. Just work on it little by little, day by day. Start now!

FIVE-MINUTE MEDITATION

Step 1   Breathe in deeeeeeeply through your nose and out through your mouth. Make an "aaahhhh" noise (like a satisfied sigh) as you breathe out.

Step 2   Envision a beautiful light of any color (blue or purple works wonderfully) encasing you in a sphere. You feel comfortable, safe, and totally relaxed.

Step 3   Continue breathing deeply. Allow all thoughts to pass without judgment; don't focus on any one thought.

Step 4   After a few minutes, envision the light of your sphere slowly shrinking into your core.

Step 5   Open your eyes and return to the present.

Intention

You've probably seen the word *intention* used quite a bit regarding witchcraft, especially spellwork. But let's take a step back: What *is* intention? In short, it describes a mental state in which you are focused on some future outcome. While mindfulness meditation is focused on the present, what is happening this second, intention is forward looking. It can be that which you seek to gain in your life, or it can be something you seek to reduce. It is focused on purposes and objectives. Your intent may include concepts such as:

- Balancing emotions
- Breaking a bad habit
- Building spiritual strength
- Business/career success
- Gaining perspective or insight
- Grounding yourself
- Improving health
- Increasing energy
- Moving on from heartbreak
- Reducing feelings of anxiety and depression
- Romantic aspirations
- Speaking up

Ask yourself: What do you intend to do to improve yourself, your circumstances, the circumstances of others, or the world at large?

I have found intent to be the most important factor in any spell I cast. When you set your intention—and truly *believe* in its power—you're setting yourself up for success after the spell is cast, because you're more likely to act on the intent.

The Basics of Spellcraft: Environmental Considerations

One of the most challenging components of witchcraft is tuning out surrounding distractions and narrowing your focus. I live in New York City, so you can probably imagine just how hectic it can become with various sounds, smells, and other assorted interruptions. The chaos is *constant*.

At times, I find it's essential to ignore what's going on outside my window and remain present in the quiet nook I've carved out for myself in my home. The space is small, but it's all I need to get in the zone.

How to Create a Witchy Space

Creating a designated spell space is important to maintain continuity and consistency in your craft. After all, spells are not intended to be one-offs, but rather, a type of ritual you're inclined to come back to repeatedly. If you set up a space, however modest, where you can work on your craft, you're more likely to return to spend more time with it.

In my small apartment, I keep a portion of the communal table open for spellwork. My tools and materials live on the altar (on top of a bookshelf) behind it. I like that I don't need much room—just some space to complete the spell—and the books behind me make for a nice setting.

If you want to create space for casting in your own home or apartment, you don't need to buy much. Just make the space a comfortable one you want to return to time and again.

How to Minimize Disturbance

Carving out the space to cast is half the battle. The other half is making sure you are not disturbed while casting. Here are some suggested ways to minimize environmental disturbances:

- Pick a time for casting when your home will be settled.
- Clean your designated spell space before the time you set aside for casting.
- If possible, put your phone on airplane mode.
- Use noise-cancelling headphones, if needed.
- A closed room generally works best if others will be present in your house or apartment at your chosen casting time.
- Hopefully, you can have someone help by minding children or pets, but if not, do your best to make sure they have what they need ahead of casting.
- Rain sounds or your preferred white noise works great for blocking small amounts of noise.

The Moon

For many witches, the moon is not just a floating orb in the sky, but an actual goddess to revere. In several neopagan spiritualities, including Wicca, the moon and its phases symbolize the triple goddess: the maiden, mother, and crone. These entities are derived from ancient cultures, such as (but not limited to) Egyptian, Hindu, and Roman. Each entity of this deity stands for phases of the moon.

The goddesses are open to interpretation according to individual or collective paths. For example, the *maiden*, who symbolizes the waxing moon phase, may represent Artemis (Greek), Diana (Roman), Isis (Egyptian), or Rhiannon (Celtic). The *mother*, who symbolizes the full moon phase, may represent Demeter (Greek), Selene (Greek), Ceres (Roman), or Danu (Celtic). The *crone*, who symbolizes the waning moon phase, may represent Hecate (Greek), Kali (Hindu), Baba Yaga (Russian), Cerridwen (Welsh), or Morrigan (Celtic).

If this seems overwhelming or confusing, don't worry: It's not necessary to view the moon as a divine entity. As a witch, however, you're likely drawn to it in some way. As you continue your journey, consider how the moon and its phases might interact with the spells you want to cast.

Here's a breakdown of what kinds of spells to perform during each broad phase of the moon:

New moon: Spells for manifesting positivity, introducing something new into your life, a spiritual reset, or a clean slate. The new moon is also a great time to take a cleansing bath. You can even cast your spell while in the tub!

Waxing moon: Cast spells for growth, increase, or reaping the seeds you've sown during the waxing moon phases.

Full moon: Almost anything goes for the full moon! The energy of the full moon can be channeled to amplify *any* spellwork. Think of ways in which you'd like to make your life "full" (through friendship, financial freedom, a wealth of peace, optimal health, romantic love, etc.). During this time, I like to cast spells relating to deity work, ancestral spells, spirit contact, and psychic enhancement spells.

Waning moon: Spells with the intention of letting go, decreasing something that doesn't positively influence your life, or eliminating that which no longer serves your enlightened purpose. Banishing, binding, and "return to sender" spells (all of which fall under the category of protection spells) are a good fit. These can include spells for cutting ties with an ex, moving on from a bad habit, banishing anxieties, protecting your house, and more.

ch.3

PROTECTION AND DEFLECTION SPELLS

Protection spells are exactly what they sound like: spells to protect you, your energy, your loved ones, and the like. Deflection spells, also known as "return to sender" spells, are a specific form of protection spell that deflect negative energy back onto the sender. Upon completion of the spell, the energy is sealed (and unable to cause further harm). All deflection spells are protection spells, but not all protection spells are deflection spells.

Nondeflection protection spells are more for everyday security and can include a broad range of protective measures. You can cast a general deflection spell for negative energy that may be headed your way, whether you suspect it or you'd just like to take a precaution. (In fact, a few witches in my coven keep a mirror on their altars for a similar purpose—to send away any bad juju that enters their space.)

I have included both types of spells in this chapter. You may cast whichever the incident or moment calls for or whatever you find calls most strongly to you. The key word for the spells in this chapter is *safeguard*. The spells are defensive to shield and safeguard your energy.

These spells—like all my spells—may be cast any time you feel called. However, if you time your spellcraft by the moon's phases, I suggest casting beneath the light of the new or waning moon.

Tip: A protection spell can be as simple as this: Paint a handheld bell black. Ring it in all corners of your house to ward off hostile spirits and toxic energy.

A Spell for Banishing Negativity

Negativity is everywhere these days. You may be experiencing negativity from others in a noticeable way, or you may secretly be the object of negative thoughts. And let's not forget the negativity of self-doubt and thoughts you direct inward. No matter where the negative energy is coming from, though, this spell can help eliminate it. Note that it can be directed toward general or specific negativity.

Materials

- Obsidian, desert rose selenite, or black tourmaline

  Note: Universal substitute clear quartz

- Incense stick, elixir or essential oil spray, or cleansing bundle

- Matches or a lighter

- Black or white candle

- Writing utensil and paper

Cleanse the area and the stone with the incense, elixir, or cleansing bundle. You may speak your intentions aloud. Carefully cleanse your aura, too, to purify yourself.

Light the candle.

Using the writing utensil and paper, draw a pentagram (star shape) on the paper. It is commonly believed that drawing the pentacle in a particular way is more effective for protection: Begin by placing your writing utensil at what will be the top of the pentacle. Draw the first line by moving to the point at the lower right. Next, draw the line to the upper left. Make the next line straight to the right. Now, draw the line to the lower left and finish by making the line going back up.

Draw a circle around the pentagram to complete the pentacle. It should look like this:

Place your burning candle on the pentacle. Hold your stone of choice.

While focusing on the flame, incant,

| *"Banish negativity here, there, and everywhere."*

Repeat this incantation four more times, for a total of five times.

When you've finished, blow out or snuff the candle (or let the candle burn out, if you prefer and can do so safely) and make a wish related to the spell's intention.

A Spell for Empath Protection

Are you an empath? Although just a few years ago, many empaths suffered in secret, now there is a growing community of like-minded people who support each other online and off. An empath, put simply, is someone who easily absorbs the energetic output of others. You may be an empath if you:

- *Become drained around others, even close friends and loved ones*
- *Become overwhelmed in crowds*
- *Feel anxious about the state of the world/humanity*
- *Feel tired after going out*
- *Prefer smaller social circles*
- *Prefer to be alone often*

Contrary to popular belief, there is such a thing as an extroverted empath (that's me!). In my case, I love to be around people whose energetic output matches mine, but I become incredibly fatigued when I'm around people—particularly strangers—whose moods clash with my own. I don't typically get along very well with cynical people; I'm very particular about my friend group. If you identify with this scenario, this spell may be for you. Cast it when you feel you need protection from the unfamiliar and/or harmful energies you encounter.

Materials

- Incense stick, elixir or essential oil spray, or cleansing bundle
- Matches or a lighter
- White candle
- Calming music

Cleanse the area with the incense, elixir, or cleansing bundle. You may speak your intentions aloud. Carefully cleanse your aura, too, to purify yourself.

Light the candle.

Play calming music. After a moment, hum along with its tune.

Close your eyes. Breathe deeply and find a rhythm in your breath. Imagine immersing yourself in a veil of violet. You're completely surrounded by this color. Perhaps it's spherical in nature, like a bubble of water. Or maybe you picture it as a soft cloak or a beaming wave of light that wraps around you and dances with your energy.

After several minutes of this visualization, open your eyes. Incant six times:

> *"I am grateful for my empathic nature,*
> *which allows me to sense the emotions of others.*
> *I call for protection against harsh moods or motives."*

Whenever you're surrounded by unfamiliar or sour energy, close your eyes and come back to your visualization of the veil of violet.

When you've finished, blow out or snuff the candle (or let the candle burn out, if you prefer and can do so safely) and make a wish related to the spell's intention.

A Jar Spell for Psychic Protection

Do you suspect someone is messing with your energy? Not every witch believes this is possible to do remotely, but if you are reading this spell, you may have a reason to believe it could be happening to you. This jar spell offers a way to trap negative energy once it comes into your home, no matter the source. Besides juniper berries, which you may need to forage or order, these ingredients are all easy to source. When arranged together, I find they look autumnal.

Materials

- Aniseed
- Juniper berries
- Sweet corn kernels
- Dried calendula
- Jar with a cloth to use as a lid
- Writing utensil and paper
- Black pepper
- Scissors

Place the aniseed, juniper berries, sweet corn kernels, and calendula into the jar.

Using the writing utensil and paper, write down your intention for psychic protection and put the paper into the jar. Sprinkle the black pepper on top.

Tip: Make it personal. Write to your deities/Spirit/the universe in prayer format.

Leave the lid off the jar, if you're able to do so safely. If this isn't feasible, cut a few 1-inch (2.5 cm) slits in the cloth and tie it on top of the jar.

Keep the jar on your altar, or wherever you meditate. Refresh the ingredients whenever it's necessary.

WHAT TO LOVE ABOUT JAR SPELLS

- Jar spells are a wonderful way to hone your intention in a visual way.
- They're portable, to a degree. They're not as portable as pouch spells, sure, but you can move them around your house if you are not sure, at first, which placement is right for them.
- Jars are compact and clean. You don't have to worry about making a mess.
- Jars can be open in some way, if you'd like them to breathe. A cloth lid with a 1-inch (2.5 cm) slit in it is a great way to let the jar stay open and mingle its energy with yours.

A Jar Spell to Protect Your House

This protection spell is broader than A Jar Spell for Psychic Protection (page 50), as it is meant to protect not only you, but also your entire home. Home is a safe, sacred space, and it's best to keep it that way. You can use this spell to protect against something in particular or as a general way to keep your home a safe space. Consider using this spell in the following situations: if you've just moved into a house and sense lingering bad energy; if your home feels stagnant; if your neighbors don't have the best intentions; or even if a guest you've invited into your home has arrived with negative energy.

You can collect the acorns yourself to add a bit more of a personal note to this spell. Dill and nutmeg are easy to source, and the black candle wax is fun. Black is a strong color for protection—it will immediately dissolve any negativity.

Materials

- Acorns
- Dried dill weed
- Whole nutmeg
- Jar with a cloth to use as a lid
- Writing utensil and paper
- Matches or a lighter
- Black candle
- Scissors
- Black paint (optional)

Place the acorns, dill, and nutmeg into the jar.

Using the writing utensil and paper, write down your intention to protect your house and put the paper into the jar.

Tip: Make it personal. Write to your deities/Spirit/the universe in prayer format.

Light the candle and carefully drip the black candle wax onto the contents of the jar, including your intention paper.

When you've finished, blow out or snuff the candle (or let the candle burn out, if you prefer and can do so safely) and make a wish related to the spell's intention.

Leave the lid off the jar, if you're able to do so safely. If this isn't feasible, cut a few 1-inch (2.5 cm) slits in the cloth and tie it on top of the jar.

Paint the jar black for added protection, if you would like. Keep the jar near your front door, if possible, or where your family hangs out most.

Tip: Make two or more jars and keep one at every entrance to your home.

USING CANDLE WAX

Spells take time to manifest—think of it like marinating food. Wax from a spell candle can be a nice way to add another element to the mix. For best results, use a tapered spell candle, not a jar candle. To drip wax on a jar spell, hold the candle by the end. Light it with a match and then hold it over the open jar. Move the candle in a counterclockwise circle if you're trying to get rid of or banish something. Move it clockwise when you want to add something to your life, such as abundance or in manifesting spells. You don't need to let too much burn down. Start with about ten drops, or whatever feels good.

A Spell for Establishing a Relationship with Spirit

This is a perfect spell for when you first begin honing your psychic abilities.

Some witches believe that casting a magick circle before beginning spellwork is key, as it serves to implement a protective, purified barrier within the magickal realm. Personally, I cast these infrequently because I believe my cleansing rituals and intentions are enough to protect me and retain the purity of my spellwork. If you're a little more superstitious, or you simply feel inclined to cast a magick circle, you're more than welcome to do so, of course.

Materials

- Amethyst, black tourmaline, or hematite

  Note: Universal substitute clear quartz

- Incense stick, elixir or essential oil spray, or cleansing bundle
- Matches or a lighter
- Black candle
- Music in 417 Hz (available on YouTube; visit mindfulnessexercises. com/417-hz-wipes-negative-energy/ for more information.)
- Headphones or speakers

Cleanse the area and the stone with the incense, elixir, or cleansing bundle. You may speak your intentions aloud; for example, "Remove that which impairs or clutters my space and my energy." Carefully cleanse your aura, too, to purify yourself.

Light the candle.

Play the music in 417 Hz. Use speakers or headphones for an amplified effect.

Bask in the music for a few minutes. As you do so, envision yourself casting a circle. Imagine a white, purple, or blue light rushing out of your aura and into the surrounding area. The light will take shape as a sphere that encompasses you, your stone, and your candles completely.

Chant one time total,

> *"My circle is cast; within it I am safe on my journey to the spirit world."*

Continue playing the music until the end of the spell. Talk to Spirit. Don't ask for anything. (Would you ask someone you just met for a favor?) Instead, focus on cultivating a positive and mutually beneficial relationship.

When you're finished, envision the light of the circle shrinking into your core. Say,

> *"Thank you, Spirit. The circle is now closed."*

When you've finished, blow out or snuff the candle (or let the candle burn out, if you prefer and can do so safely) and make a wish related to the spell's intention.

A Spell for Setting Personal Boundaries

Maybe it's a co-worker or maybe it's a family member, but most of us have someone in our lives who has trouble respecting boundaries. Yet, confrontation can be hard and it also may not accomplish everything you wished for. This is a spell to help with personal boundaries, especially if you have trouble addressing them in person.

Materials

- Hematite, fire agate, and/or pyrite

  Note: Universal substitute clear quartz

- Incense stick, elixir or essential oil spray, or cleansing bundle
- White candle
- Table salt
- Matches or a lighter

Cleanse the area and the stone(s) with the incense, elixir, or cleansing bundle. You may speak your intentions aloud. Carefully cleanse your aura, too, to purify yourself.

Place the candle on a hard surface. Pour a small circle of salt around the candle.

Light the candle.

Place the stone(s) around the outside of the salt circle.

While focusing on the candle's flame, say,

| *"I protect, I deflect, my boundaries are set."*

Incant this phrase five more times, for a total of six times.

Take a few deep breaths.

When you've finished, blow out or snuff the candle (or let the candle burn out, if you prefer and can do so safely) and make a wish related to the spell's intention. You may leave the salt circle in place as long as you'd like.

A Pouch Spell for Protection When You're Out and About

I love pouch spells because the pouch can go anywhere you go. Toss it into your purse or backpack—or a suitcase for longer journeys. Pouch spells are perfect for empaths, who often suck up the energy of others. Even though I'm extroverted, I find I can be thrown off by absorbing the energy of others. You probably know this feeling if you have ever run into someone having a bad day and it spilled over and made your day worse. This pouch spell can help with that problem, protecting you from anything negative that comes your way. The intention you write during this spell is intentionally left open. In this case, it is more powerful for you to craft, in your own words, the intention behind the protection you wish to receive.

Materials

- Black tourmaline
- Incense stick, elixir or essential oil spray, or cleansing bundle
- Cumin seeds
- Whole nutmeg
- Raw rice
- Pouch
- Writing utensil and paper
- Twine

Cleanse the area and the stone with the incense, elixir, or cleansing bundle. You may speak your intentions aloud. Carefully cleanse your aura, too, to purify yourself.

Place the cumin seeds, nutmeg, and rice into the pouch.

Using the writing utensil and paper, write down your intention for protection wherever you go. Fold the paper around the black tourmaline (you may tie it with twine, if you prefer) and add the bundle to the pouch.

Tip: Make it personal. Write to your deities/Spirit/the universe in prayer format.

Tie the pouch closed and keep it on your person when you travel outside the home. Whenever you feel unsafe, open the pouch and take a deep breath in. (Make sure your nose is a safe distance away from the contents— please don't accidentally inhale the ingredients!) Refresh the ingredients whenever you feel it's necessary. Dispose when you believe the spell is complete. You may thank Spirit, the universe, or your deities as you do so.

A Mirror Spell to Constantly Deflect Negative Energy

As I mentioned at the beginning of this chapter, there is a difference between protection spells and deflection spells. This spell is the latter. Also known as a "return to sender" spell, it is meant to constantly shield against negativity. The mirror serves to reflect negative energy sent your way back to its sender, creating an effective barrier because the energy is unable to penetrate the reflective surface.

Materials

- Incense stick, elixir or essential oil spray, or cleansing bundle
- Mirror you find aesthetically pleasing (it can be one you own or a new one)
- Decorative materials (optional)

Cleanse the area with the incense, elixir, or cleansing bundle. You may speak your intentions aloud. Carefully cleanse your aura, too, to purify yourself. Cleanse the mirror with the incense, elixir, or cleansing bundle.

Optional: Decorate the mirror how you see fit. You may adorn it with flowers, herbs, crystals, drawings, painted sigils, or whatever comes to mind.

Bless your mirror with this incantation, eight times in total:

> *"Mirror, I ask that you deflect*
> *all that may affect*
> *my energy negatively.*
> *Mirror, I ask that you bounce back*
> *every single attack*
> *on my loved ones, my home, and me."*

Place the mirror on your altar indefinitely to deflect negative energy. Cleanse the mirror once a week.

WHEN TO CHOOSE DEFLECTION SPELLS

In my opinion, a witch should only choose to cast a deflection spell when they believe someone intends to cause harm. There are numerous examples of this potential, including online trolls (I'm no stranger to these), a friendship gone sour, a toxic former relationship, or resentment at your workplace or school. If you don't truly believe you're under psychic attack, it's probably unnecessary to cast a deflection spell, and it could potentially drain your well of magickal energy. This certainly isn't a life-altering risk, however.

The Mirror Spell to Constantly Deflect Negative Energy (page 56) is a great option for overall protection, if you have a hunch someone is throwing unpleasant energy your way—or will be, if you've divined a future attack. I tend not to cast deflection spells because I'm confident in my natural ability to deflect energy directed at me by rising above and choosing to ignore the noise. Plus, a sea salt bath, black tourmaline, and a black candle go a long way to protect!

As I always say: To each their own. Follow your witchy intuition and cast whichever spell best suits your needs based on what your gut tells you.

A New Moon Potion Spell for Protection

Many witches are obsessed with the full moon. It makes sense, as the full moon is not only powerful but visually impressive. But just because you can't see the new moon in the same way as a full moon doesn't mean it's any less powerful. Personally, I love the new moon. I view it as a clean slate, erasing whatever you want to be rid of and letting you start new.

Although this is a potion spell, it does not make a potion that is meant to be consumed. I admit, I thought this was weird when I first did it, but then kept coming back to it. Think of it more like a jar spell, or perhaps like a glass of water left out by your bed at night, which can absorb anything harmful while you sleep.

Materials

- Smoky quartz crystal

  Note: Universal substitute clear quartz

- Sea salt (ethically sourced)

- Cinnamon sticks or ground cinnamon

- Glass jar

- Purified (filtered) water

- Spoon or other stirring device

Place the smoky quartz, sea salt, and cinnamon into the jar.

Pour purified water over the contents of the jar.

Hold the jar. Pray your intention for protection.

Set the jar out overnight during the new moon. Leave it to collect the energy of the new moon for at least 12 hours.

Stirring the potion clockwise, incant six times total,

> *"Protect this house and those who live in it."*

Note: When I cast this spell, I prefer stirring clockwise because I see this spell as adding protection to my life. However, it may feel more natural to stir counterclockwise if you feel the spell is removing negative energy.

Put the jar on your altar for protection until the next month's new moon, when you can refresh the ingredients.

ch.4

ABUNDANCE
SPELLS

To understand abundance spells, let's look at the word *abundance*. It can mean a large amount of something, or it can refer to the feeling that whatever you are measuring is plentiful (even if the number is not high). Many people think of money and wealth first when they picture abundance, yet so many concepts fit into this idea. For example, do you feel like you have enough friends, or would you like them to be more plentiful?

This chapter's spells are unified by the idea of abundance. They focus on what you'd like to amplify, the kind of wealth you hope to acquire (monetary or otherwise), and that which you strive to make plentiful in your life.

Another key word for this chapter is *attraction*. What favors, assets, or blessings do you hope to attract? Maybe you already have something in mind, or maybe browsing this chapter will give you a few ideas.

These spells—like nearly all my spells—may be cast any time you feel called. But if you time your spellcraft by the moon's phases, I suggest casting beneath the light of the full or waxing moon.

A Spell to Increase Gratitude

Have you ever noticed how many spells are centered on asking for something? Even deflection spells are asking for a specific action. This spell is for doing the opposite—expressing gratitude. Perhaps you already do something similar: Many people like to write down a few things they are thankful for at the end of each day as part of a gratitude practice. If you are new to this, don't be intimidated. At first, people often think gratitude is only for "big" things. But you can be thankful for something as small as the last meal you enjoyed or something cute your dog did. What little things in your day make you happy?

Materials

- Green aventurine, tiger's eye, and/or malachite

  Note: Universal substitute clear quartz

- Incense stick, elixir or essential oil spray, or cleansing bundle

- Matches or a lighter

- White candle

- Writing utensil and paper

Cleanse the area and the stone(s) with the incense, elixir, or cleansing bundle. You may speak your intentions aloud; for example, "Free my atmosphere of that which does not raise me." Carefully cleanse your aura, too, to purify yourself.

Light the candle.

Using the writing utensil and paper, write down five things you're grateful for and why you are grateful for them.

Place the stone(s) atop the paper.

Draw your attention to the flame of the candle, then incant three times total,

> *"Thank you, [deity/Spirit/universe], for my riches are grand;*
> *thank you, [deity/Spirit/universe], for I'm blessed by your hand;*
> *thank you, [deity/Spirit/universe], for that which will come;*
> *thank you, [deity/Spirit/universe], I forget not where I'm from."*

Take a few deep breaths.

When you've finished, blow out or snuff the candle (or let the candle burn out, if you prefer and can do so safely) and make a wish related to the spell's intention.

A Spell for Reviving Love Energy

I believe love energy is the purest of energies, locked within our heart-mind connection. We all have a reserve of this positive, loving energy. Think about a baby—pure, happy, and loving. We all still have that energy somewhere inside, but it's often lost, buried beneath negative energy or other cosmic muck we collect in our day-to-day lives. This spell is meant to help you free that natural light source within, so it may radiate inward and outward. Try to unearth your positive energy. As you craft this spell, think about innocence.

Materials

- Rose quartz and/or rainbow fluorite

  Note: Universal substitute clear quartz

- Incense stick, elixir or essential oil spray, or cleansing bundle

- Brewed hibiscus, lemon balm, or juniper berry tea

- Matches or a lighter

- Pink or white candle

Cleanse the area and the stone(s) with the incense, elixir, or cleansing bundle. You may speak your intentions aloud; for example, "Free my atmosphere of that which does not raise me." Carefully cleanse your aura, too, to purify yourself.

Pour the tea and take a sip.

Light the candle.

Hold the stone(s) in your palms, facing up, and incant seven times total,

> *"Spirit—transmute my energy into love;*
> *may it flow in, through, and around me.*
> *I seek abundance of love energy."*

Drink the tea. (No need to chug it; consume it at whatever pace suits you as you contemplate.)

When you've finished, blow out or snuff the candle (or let the candle burn out, if you prefer and can do so safely) and make a wish related to the spell's intention.

A Spell for Self-Love

Self-love is hard. Please don't go into this spell thinking you can cast it and it will fix everything. It won't—because self-love is a practice. Chances are that this spell may even feel weird at first. Do you really believe what you are saying? You may not, the first time you say it—or the tenth. But cast this spell enough and you will eventually believe (fake it 'til you make it!). And even if you don't love yourself after casting a few times, you may at least notice a small change. Perhaps you don't hate yourself or just come to a more neutral space. That is good, too! Overcompensating can be a good way to end up in the middle, and being okay with yourself is definitely okay.

Materials

- Kunzite, rose quartz, and/or rhodochrosite

  Note: Universal substitute clear quartz

- Incense stick, elixir or essential oil spray, or cleansing bundle
- Writing utensil and paper
- Jar with a lid
- Dried apricot, rosemary, sugar, and/or dried beets (optional)
- Matches or a lighter
- Pink or white candle for sealing the jar (optional)

Cleanse the area and the stone(s) with the incense, elixir, or cleansing bundle. You may speak your intentions aloud; for example, "Suffuse the atmosphere with joy." Carefully cleanse your aura, too, to purify yourself.

Rip or cut the paper into nine pieces.

Using the writing utensil, on each piece of paper, write down a reason you're lovable. Be thorough. For example: "I'm compassionate, even when it would be easy to turn away." "I don't shy away from challenges." "I'm the peacemaker among my friends and family."

When you're finished, put your reflections into the jar.

Hold the stone(s) and say,

> "I am love and love is me;
> I am worthy of all good things."

Incant the phrase eight more times, for a total of nine times.

Put the stone(s) and any optional material you have chosen in the jar.

Put the lid on the jar. Optionally, seal it with pink or white candle wax. Display the jar where it will draw your attention for as long as you wish, or until you feel compelled to change the ingredients.

A Spell for Improving Body Image

This is a spell to help you feel good about your body. It is a vessel you must cherish, yet how do you do that when your body image fluctuates constantly and is too often at a low point? Like A Spell for Self-Love (page 66), this is a spell that must be practiced often, like a sport or an instrument. Acceptance is the goal.

I have talked to many who find this spell hard because you are forced to face yourself. You have to look your demons in the eye. I admit, when I do this spell, I sometimes hate myself for whatever I am struggling with, whether it's physical or mental. I am not a therapist, but I have learned that it's a good idea to accept what you can . . . even when you can't accept everything. Work on accepting one thing at a time, if you're struggling with this spell. Work up to the whole you.

Materials

- Rose quartz and/or citrine

  Note: Universal substitute/add-on clear quartz

- Incense stick, elixir or essential oil spray, or cleansing bundle
- Matches or a lighter
- Pink candle
- Writing utensil and paper
- Mirror

Cleanse the area and the stone(s) with the incense, elixir, or cleansing bundle. You may speak your intentions aloud; for example, "Raise me up within this space." Carefully cleanse your aura, too, to purify yourself.

Light the candle.

Using the writing utensil and paper, record four features you love about your body and how they connect to your craft. For example, "My hands, because they make culinary magick," or "My eyes, because they are perceptive and discerning in a world of chaos." You may be as specific as you like.

Hold the stone(s) and look in a mirror. Say (being as specific as you like),

> *"My beauty extends far beyond the surface.*
> *My practice fuels my positive self-image.*
> *I am eyes, because they are perceptive and discerning in a world of chaos."*

When you've finished, blow out or snuff the candle (or let the candle burn, if you prefer and can do so safely) and thank the universe for your abundant blessings.

WITCHY TIP: BE DIVINE

Make a habit of holding your body in the highest regard—after all, it houses the brilliant mind responsible for your craft! If you treat your body like divinity, divine things will happen upon you. So: Eat right. Exercise. Care for your skin. Drink water (and then drink some more water). And, of course, rest when you're tired.

A Jar Spell for Creativity

Orange is my favorite color: It is loaded with creativity and energy. Red and yellow can be too intense at times (Have you ever noticed how hard it can be to wear a yellow shirt?!), but never orange. If pure orange is too bright, you can find a shade that is soft and beautiful, like a faded, dry orange peel left in the sun. This whole spell is themed around orange, both the color and the fruit. The fruit brings fresh energy: You can eat it and then use the aromatic peel in this spell.

Materials

- Carnelian, yellow calcite, or citrine

  Note: Universal substitute/add-on clear quartz

- Incense stick, elixir or essential oil spray, or cleansing bundle

- Orange peel

- Orchid

- Ground paprika

- Jar with a cloth to use as a lid

- Writing utensil and paper

- Scissors

Cleanse the area and the stone with the incense, elixir, or cleansing bundle. You may speak your intentions aloud. Carefully cleanse your aura, too, to purify yourself.

Place the orange peel, orchid, and paprika into the jar.

Using the writing utensil and paper, write down your intention for creativity. Fold the paper around the carnelian and add the bundle to the jar.

Tip: Make it personal. Write to your deities/Spirit/the universe in prayer format.

Leave the lid off the jar, if you're able to do so safely. If this isn't feasible, cut a few 1-inch (2.5 cm) slits in the cloth and tie it on top of the jar.

Keep the jar near wherever you work. Refresh the ingredients whenever you feel it's necessary. Dispose when you believe the spell is complete. You may thank Spirit, the universe, or your deities as you do so.

A Jar Spell for Increased Energy

Many witches are attuned to their sense of smell. Incense is a popular way to quickly change the scent in a space, but jar spells can be aromatic as well. Some aromas in this spell may bring you back to a certain memory or mood. (And if you want to boost the scent of this spell or add to its complexity, add essential oils, such as lemon. Just use care not to get oils on a raw stone, as they can mingle with its properties and ruin it.)

Mint can be a refreshing and awakening herb or a sleepy herb. Mint tea may be nice in the evening, but in this spell, we are channeling its freshness and awakening properties.

Materials

- Citrine

  Note: Universal substitute clear quartz

- Incense stick, elixir or essential oil spray, or cleansing bundle
- Mint
- Sunflower
- Cantaloupe
- Fennel seed
- Jar with a cloth to use as a lid
- Writing utensil and paper
- Scissors

Cleanse the area and the stone with the incense, elixir, or cleansing bundle. You may speak your intentions aloud. Carefully cleanse your aura, too, to purify yourself.

Place the mint, sunflower, cantaloupe, and fennel seed into the jar.

Using the writing utensil and paper, write down your intention for increased energy. Fold the paper around the citrine and place the bundle in the jar.

Tip: Make it personal. Write to your deities/Spirit/the universe in prayer format.

Leave the lid off the jar, if you're able to do so safely. If this isn't feasible, cut a few 1-inch (2.5 cm) slits in the cloth and tie it on top of the jar.

Keep the jar near wherever you work. Refresh the contents whenever it's necessary.

A Spell for Compassion

Sometimes you get hurt in life. Life throws obstacles at you, or perhaps, you get caught up in negative feelings for a person—as at the end of a relationship. Especially if you are a water sign (Cancer, Pisces, Scorpio), you may find it easy to build walls after getting hurt. Yet, if you do, you will eventually succumb to an attachment-avoidant nature. You will avoid love at all costs—and nobody wants to live that way. It's okay if you're hurt or have baggage. Don't avoid your vulnerability. Instead, try to channel compassion for whoever or whatever situation has hurt you.

Materials

- Rhodonite and/or lepidolite

  Note: Universal substitute clear quartz

- Incense stick, elixir or essential oil spray, or cleansing bundle

- Roman chamomile essential oil, diluted in a carrier oil (important: test a patch on your skin before using it to check for any negative reactions)

- Diffuser (optional)

- Matches or a lighter

- Pink candle

Cleanse the area and the stone(s) with the incense, elixir, or cleansing bundle. You may speak your intentions aloud; for example, "Remove this space of that which does not bring joy and good health." Carefully cleanse your aura, too, to purify yourself.

Place 3 or 4 drops of diluted Roman chamomile essential oil on your wrists, chest, and upper back. You can also diffuse it throughout the room, if you like.

Light the candle.

Holding the stone(s) over your heart chakra, which is in the center of your chest, chant four times total,

> *"I am gentle, generous, and gracious.*
> *I respond kindly to myself;*
> *I respond kindly to others.*
> *I forgive myself; I forgive others.*
> *I diffuse negativity with my impenetrably radiant and loving spirit."*

Close your eyes. Visualize a green light glowing in the middle of your chest. Your heart chakra is open, balanced, and receptive. It is a natural filter; it is a vessel for that which is wholesome. It is love. YOU are love.

Take a few deep breaths.

When you've finished, blow out or snuff the candle (or let the candle burn out, if you prefer and can do so safely) and make a wish related to the spell's intention.

A Spell to Make New Friends

When you're in high school or college, it's easy to make friends. But as adults, we often don't have that same sense of community—especially if we work from home. Making friends can become a weird thing to navigate. Some people may be embarrassed to admit they don't have a ton of friends.

I'm not afraid to say there have been times as an adult when I was in a new place and had zero friends. What helped me break through was focus and confidence in myself. This is a spell to help you harness that intent and confidence and to attract the right energy. Whether you have one friend or 100, don't be embarrassed if you're looking for more.

Materials

- Lapis lazuli, rose quartz, and/or carnelian

  Note: Universal substitute clear quartz
- Incense stick, elixir or essential oil spray, or cleansing bundle
- Matches or a lighter
- Orange candle
- Writing utensil and paper

Cleanse the area and the stone(s) with the incense, elixir, or cleansing bundle. You may speak your intentions aloud; for example, "Raise my vibrations." Carefully cleanse your aura, too, to purify yourself.

Light the candle.

Using the writing utensil and paper, write down, "I manifest new friendships."

Place the stone(s) on the paper.

Incant three times total,

> *"I am worthy of fulfilling companionship; I draw in those who seek that which I seek."*

When you've finished, blow out or snuff the candle (or let the candle burn out, if you prefer and can do so safely) and make a wish related to the spell's intent. Thank the universe for your abundant blessings.

A Jar Spell to Attract New Friends

Although there is A Spell to Make New Friends (page 74), I have made a jar spell for this concept as well. There are so many spells out there for love and not all that many for friendship. Yet friendship is just as important as love—for some, it could even be more important or desirable. A jar spell provides an anchor in your home for this thought and may help you connect with new acquaintances who enter your home.

In this spell, a pink or white rose represents self-love and pure energy. Apple is a powerful fruit that stands for a lot of things, including love and friendship. And lemon balm has a soothing, calm energy— if you want to make new friends, you have to make sure you are in a place where you are ready to accept new energy.

Materials

- Malachite or blue chalcedony

  Note: Universal substitute clear quartz

- Incense stick, elixir or essential oil spray, or cleansing bundle
- Dried apple
- Lemon balm
- Pink or white rose
- Jar with a cloth to use as a lid
- Writing utensil and paper
- Scissors

Cleanse the area and the stone with the incense, elixir, or cleansing bundle. You may speak your intentions aloud. Carefully cleanse your aura, too, to purify yourself.

Place the dried apple, lemon balm, and rose into the jar.

Using the writing utensil and paper, write down your intention for new friendships. Fold the paper around the malachite and place the bundle in the jar.

Tip: Make it personal. Write to your deities/Spirit/the universe in prayer format.

Leave the lid off the jar, if you're able to do so safely. If this isn't feasible, cut a few 1-inch (2.5 cm) slits in the cloth and tie it on top of the jar.

Keep the jar near the entrance of your house, or wherever you tend to welcome people into your home. Refresh the ingredients whenever you feel it's necessary. Dispose when you believe the spell is complete. You may thank Spirit, the universe, or your deities as you do so.

A Spell to Enchant the Object of Your Affection

People have differing opinions about love spells. Some people think they're unethical, but I think love spells don't do anything that is not meant to be done. I don't believe they can make someone love you (or like you) if they otherwise never would. Rather, a love spell may have the ability to open someone's eyes to a possibility they did not realize existed—even if it was right in front of them. It also helps you focus on your intentions toward another and is likely to increase your confidence when interacting with them—and confidence is an attractive quality. The way I see it, the worst that can happen is that your spell does not work. And even that is for the best, as it means the person was not meant for you. Your search for love can continue in a more productive direction.

Materials

- Garnet and/or ruby

  Note: Universal substitute clear quartz

- Incense stick, elixir or essential oil spray, or cleansing bundle
- Stimulating music
- Matches or a lighter
- Red candle
- Writing utensil and paper

Cleanse the area and the stone(s) with the incense, elixir, or cleansing bundle. You may speak your intentions aloud; for example, "Clarify and sensualize the atmosphere." Carefully cleanse your aura, too, to purify yourself.

Play the music.

Light the candle.

Using the writing utensil and paper, write down the name of the object of your affection.

Holding the stone(s), incant five times total,

> "I am a force of arousal, romance, and radical desire.
> I draw thee in, [Name], so you may awaken to my magnetism."

Place the stone(s) true south of the candle.

Kiss the paper to activate the enchantment and place it beneath the stone(s).

When you've finished, blow out or snuff the candle (or let the candle burn out, if you prefer and can do so safely) and make a wish related to the spell's intention.

Sleep soundly. The next morning, clean up the paper and stone. Consider putting it on your altar or in another sweet spot.

A Spell for Increasing Romantic Appeal

What makes this spell different from A Spell to Enchant the Object of Your Affection (page 76)? Unlike that spell, which includes another person, this spell is focused internally. That means you don't have anyone in mind as a love match, but you want to make yourself more desirable. When you're trying to date, you can easily get nervous and even forget how to flirt. (Though for air signs—Aquarius, Gemini, Libra—flirting comes naturally.) Some people get nervous at the idea of romance. This spell can help draw out the playful romantic energy you have within you.

Materials

- Incense stick, elixir or essential oil spray, or cleansing bundle
- Red garments
- Matches or a lighter
- Red candle
- Writing utensil and paper

Cleanse the area with the incense, elixir, or cleansing bundle. You may speak your intentions aloud; for example, "Open the gateway to romance." Carefully cleanse your aura, too, to purify yourself.

Shed the day's clothing, and dress yourself in red garments.

Light the candle.

Using the writing utensil and paper, write down, "I am the fire to which suitors are drawn. I radiate love, warmth, comfort, and passion." Fold the paper and hold it in your hands.

Close your eyes, visualize your magnetism, and whisper,

> *"Come hither. Come hither. Come hither."*

Open your eyes. Blow out or snuff the candle (or let the candle burn, if you prefer and can do so safely) and make a wish related to the spell's intention.

Place the paper beneath your pillow. Do not dispose of it until morning.

A Pouch Spell for Love

If you are in the process of finding love, there is a good chance you are not sitting at home! So, what's better than a pouch spell to bring with you when you go out? I've found this spell can help quell your nerves, especially in those five minutes before a date starts. That said, you can use it whenever you go out with friends. Maybe you will sense a love connection nearby, at which point you can shake it up to help activate the spell.

Materials

- Rose quartz
  Note: Universal substitute clear quartz
- Incense stick, elixir or essential oil spray, or cleansing bundle
- Dried apricot
- Dried gardenia or hibiscus
- Basil
- Cloth pouch
- Writing utensil and paper
- Twine

Cleanse the area with the incense, elixir, or cleansing bundle. You may speak your intentions aloud. Carefully cleanse your aura, too, to purify yourself.

Place the apricot, gardenia, and basil into the pouch.

Using the writing utensil and paper, write down your intention for love. Fold the paper around the rose quartz (you may tie it with twine, if you prefer) and add the bundle to the pouch.

Tie the pouch closed and keep it on your altar or bring it with you on dates.

Shake the pouch when you sense a love connection nearby. Refresh the ingredients whenever you feel it's necessary. Dispose when you believe the spell is complete. You may thank Spirit, the universe, or your deities as you do so.

An Abundance Spell for the Full Moon

Most people's sense of sight is their strongest sense—and few things are as appealing to our sense of sight as the full moon. (After all, very few have been able to touch it!) When you step outside on a clear full-moon night, you can see the big, beautiful moon in all its glory. Harnessing this excitement is a good power to have.

As you consider the full moon, think about abundance and whatever you want to be most full in your life—this could be love, money, or something else. (The new moon is more for protection; it is viewed as black, dissolving, and releasing.) The full moon is all about honing, focusing on what you want your life to be full of. Anything goes—the full moon is that powerful. What do you want in your life? What would truly make it full?

Note: This spell may be cast the day or night before, during, or just after the full moon. Go with what feels right for you.

Materials

- Labradorite, selenite, or moonstone

  Note: Universal substitute clear quartz

- Incense stick, elixir or essential oil spray, or cleansing bundle

- Brewed ginger tea

- Matches or a lighter

- White or silver candle

Cleanse the area and the stone with the incense, elixir, or cleansing bundle. You may speak your intentions aloud; for example, "Free my atmosphere of that which does not raise me." Carefully cleanse your aura, too, to purify yourself.

Pour the ginger tea and sip it.

Light the candle.

Holding the stone, close your eyes and say what you hope to manifest from the full moon.

When you've finished, blow out or snuff the candle (or let the candle burn out, if you prefer and can do so safely) and thank the universe for your abundant blessings.

A Spell for Getting Hired

This is a spell to help you find a new job, whether within your industry or in a new field. It's all about confidence, as people tend to get down on themselves during the job-hunting process, which can be trying and tedious. You're waiting on someone else to do something, and you know they're judging you. It's hard to accept that so much is out of your hands! This spell is a way to calm down and instill patience. It helps you feel less powerless, take the power back, and banish your fear.

Materials

- Green aventurine and/or sodalite

  Note: Universal substitute clear quartz

- Incense stick, elixir or essential oil spray, or cleansing bundle

- Matches or a lighter

- Green candle

- Pecans

Cleanse the area and the stone(s) with the incense, elixir, or cleansing bundle. You may speak your intentions aloud; for example, "Free my atmosphere of that which does not raise me." Carefully cleanse your aura, too, to purify yourself.

Light the candle. Place the green aventurine true north of the candle.

Lay the pecans in a circle around the candle and stone(s).

Incant,

> "I seek new opportunities in my career;
>   help me rise above; banish all fear."

Note: You may eat the pecans, or leave them on display.

When you've finished, blow out or snuff the candle (or let the candle burn out, if you prefer and can do so safely) and make a wish related to the spell's intention.

A Spell for Attaining Financial Freedom

This is a simpler spell than A Potion Spell for Money Manifestation (page 84) to help you manifest money. You may try one or both of these money manifestation spells; see which feels more powerful to you! To me, this one is less urgent—it's less about now and more about the long game. What does financial freedom mean to you? Perhaps you're working on saving money for a luxurious vacation or an early retirement. That's what this spell is all about.

To me, financial freedom is not having to worry about money. Everyone wants that future. To be clear: You can't just cast this spell and expect to have no debt, but it will help you focus your intention in that direction. It puts money top of mind, so you'll work hard for it.

Materials

- Pyrite or green aventurine

  Note: Universal substitute clear quartz
- Incense stick, elixir or essential oil spray, or cleansing bundle
- Matches or a lighter
- Green candle
- Writing utensil and paper

Cleanse the area and the stone with the incense, elixir, or cleansing bundle. You may speak your intentions aloud; for example, "Cleanse and uplift." Carefully cleanse your aura, too, to purify yourself.

Light the candle.

Using the writing utensil and paper, write down the amount of money you wish to secure in the next year.

Hold the stone in your palms, facing upward, and incant four times total,

> *"I attract riches through my craft;*
> *I hone my personal power through my craft.*
> *I am well-equipped for financial success."*

Take five deep breaths. Imagine inhaling that which helps you achieve your goal and exhaling that which hinders your goal.

When you've finished, blow out or snuff the candle (or let the candle burn out, if you prefer and can do so safely) and make a wish related to the spell's intention.

A Potion Spell for Money Manifestation

This is a comprehensive spell to help you manifest money. As such, it does have a lot of ingredients compared to some other spells in this book, but fortunately, they are common ingredients and easy to find.

Picture a cauldron bubbling away. You can just keep throwing these ingredients in—you're using fire and water, and it feels powerful to use your own money as well. Try to focus and bring high energy to casting this spell.

Materials

- Golden rutilated quartz and/or citrine (ensure they are water-safe)

  Note: Universal substitute clear quartz

- Incense stick, elixir or essential oil spray, or cleansing bundle
- Matches or a lighter
- Green candle
- Clean coins
- Small cast-iron cauldron, bowl, or pot
- Purified (filtered) water
- Spoon

Cleanse the area and the stone(s) with the incense, elixir, or cleansing bundle. You may speak your intentions aloud; for example, "Expel that which does not serve me." Carefully cleanse your aura, too, to purify yourself.

Light the candle.

Place the coins in the cauldron and fill it with purified water. Add your stone(s).

Using a spoon, stir the mixture clockwise. As you do so, incant six times total,

> *"Money, money, come to me;*
> *money, money, set me free.*
>
> *Money, money, grow and grow;*
> *money, money, flow and flow."*

When you've finished, blow out or snuff the candle (or let the candle burn out, if you prefer and can do so safely) and make a wish related to the spell's intention.

Leave the mixture overnight.

Optional: Place some of the water in a small jar the next day. You can leave this on your altar until you feel it's time to dispose of it.

THRIFTY TIP: MAKE THE MOST OF YOUR CANDLES

Don't want to use an entire candle for one spell? (If you're like me, you cast too many spells for this to be a feasible option.) That's okay. Blow it out. As you do so, close your eyes and make a wish related to the spell's intention. You can also thank the fire element afterward.

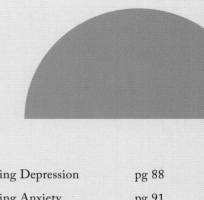

ch.5

HEALING/HEALTH SPELLS

I am not a doctor. Seek medical help if you need it. Witchcraft is not opposed to science. These spells are not a substitute for proper medical attention or therapy.

That said, sometimes you want to help yourself, or another, in any way you can. Spells are a wonderful way to practice self-care and try to improve your health by keeping it top of mind. Spells can set your mind on a new track, focused on something you want to work on, and can lead to other improvements through intention into a specific area.

When it comes to another that is ailing, spells are a strong way to communicate you are thinking about them and supporting them. (I have done this with my grandmother.) Whether or not they believe the spells will work, I am confident they will appreciate the thoughts and intentions on their behalf.

A Spell for Reducing Depression

I don't mind sharing that I have been diagnosed with, take medication for, and go to therapy for depression. It's an issue I struggle with daily. So, I can say that this spell is in no way a replacement for the other things you need to do for your mental health. But even with medication and therapy, you can have a slump. I think anything that can help bring you out of a funk and, potentially, make a lost day more productive is a good thing.

You'll notice I use blue in this spell. Although yellow represents happiness and might be the more expected choice, blue is calm and I see it as a color to turn to when you need help validating your feelings. It lets you know it's okay to have a tough time rather than correct it.

There is a journaling component to this spell, and it should not be done quickly. You should stop and consider what might lift your feelings of depression. It's symbolic when you rip up the paper. Taking charge and taking back your power is what it's all about.

Materials

- Moss agate, smoky quartz, and/or obsidian

  Note: Universal substitute clear quartz

- Incense stick, elixir or essential oil spray in juniper, lavender, rosemary, mugwort, or mullein, and/or a selenite wand for purifying

- Blue candle

- Matches or a lighter

- Writing utensil and paper

Cleanse the area and the stone(s) with the incense or elixir. You may speak your intentions aloud; for example, "Flush the atmosphere of that which ails me." Carefully cleanse your aura, too, to purify yourself. If you're using a selenite wand, wave it around your spell space and your aura slowly and intentionally.

Intuitively arrange your stone(s) around the candle, then light the candle.

Using your writing utensil and paper, write down the source(s) of your depression—for example, negative thought patterns, a difficult relationship, a toxic work or home environment, or a deficiency/excess of something.

When you've finished writing, rip up the paper and, as you do so, incant nine times total,

> *"I dispel that which depresses me."*

Repeat the incantation as many times as needed until you've finished tearing up the paper.

Note: If you have a cast-iron cauldron or pot, carefully burn the paper in it.

On another scrap of paper, list the ways in which you'll minimize or eliminate the source(s) of your depression—for example, changing your thought patterns, distancing yourself from a difficult relationship, taking leave of a toxic work or home environment, and gaining/reducing something.

When you've finished, blow out or snuff the candle (or let the candle burn out, if you prefer and can do so safely) and make a wish related to the spell's intention.

Keep the text somewhere safe for future reference. Apply your own advice to your life.

A Spell for Reducing Anxiety

This is a spell to help reduce feelings of anxiety. You'll notice this is the same format as A Spell for Reducing Depression (page 88), but it utilizes different stones, colors, and materials, as you are focusing on a different feeling here. In fact, A Spell for Reducing Fatigue (page 96) is the third in this series of spells. Take a look at all three spells and see which one calls to you to help bring you back to a neutral state.

When I do readings, I sometimes hear surprise at the results. More often, though, I hear things like, "Yeah, I know that. . . . I think I just needed to hear it from someone else." I don't believe this is always the case. When you know what you need, sometimes realizing it on your own can be just as—or more—powerful than being told by someone else.

Materials

- Fluorite, amethyst, and/ or black kyanite

  Note: Universal substitute clear quartz

- Incense stick, elixir or essential oil spray in juniper, lavender, rosemary, mugwort, or mullein, and/or a selenite wand

- Pink candle

- Matches or a lighter

- Writing utensil and paper

Cleanse the area and the stone(s) with the incense or elixir. You may speak your intentions aloud; for example, "Imbue my atmosphere with that which elevates me." Carefully cleanse your aura, too, to purify yourself. If you're using a selenite wand, wave it around your spell space and your aura slowly and intentionally.

Intuitively arrange your stone(s) around the candle, then light the candle.

Using your writing utensil and paper, write down the source(s) of your anxiety—for example, negative self-talk, a health condition, unknown outcomes, a troublesome circumstance, or an environment or relationship that dims your light.

Rip up the paper and, as you do so, incant,

> *"I dispel that which causes me anxiety."*

Repeat the incantation as many times as needed until you've finished tearing up the paper.

On another scrap of paper, list the ways in which you'll minimize or eliminate the source(s) of your anxiety—for example, employing positive self-talk, seeking to remedy a health condition, practicing peace within the unknown, simplifying a complicated circumstance, and departing an environment or relationship that doesn't serve you.

When you've finished, blow out or snuff the candle (or let the candle burn out, if you prefer and can do so safely) and make a wish related to the spell's intention.

Keep the text somewhere safe for future reference. Apply your own advice to your circumstances.

A Potion Spell for Inner Healing

Perhaps you have seen water bottles with crystals in them for sale. They are usually expensive, and my two cents is that the Thrifty Witch way of achieving the same thing is better. After all, when you infuse the water yourself with a crystal you have found, or selected yourself, you are making the effects more powerful.

Not to mention, this spell is extremely easy and the materials are quick to source. I like to use filtered water to enhance the feeling of purity—there is nothing else in it like there may be in tap water. I like using clear quartz in this spell, as it is something most witches have and it is safe to use in this application. (If you substitute another stone, make sure to research what you use, as some stones leach harmful materials in water or are not water-safe.)

Materials

- Clean medium-large or large clear quartz
- Glass
- Purified (filtered) water
- Eco-friendly straw (such as metal or bamboo)

Place the clear quartz into a glass.

Fill the glass with water.

Hold the glass and pray your intention. Visualize a white light healing you from inside out.

Put the glass in your refrigerator for a few hours.

Drink all the water using a straw (so you don't choke). Drink slowly and intentionally. Take the clear quartz out of the glass and place it on your altar.

HOW TO CLEAN A STONE

If you've collected clear quartz from a river, it is okay to wash it for up to 1 minute with soapy water. But if you know the stone is already clean, simply rinse it in warm water. Alternately, you can let it soak in a mixture of a handful of sea salt and water for an hour or so. No matter how you clean the stone, always rinse it well before and after use.

A Jar Spell for Emotional Healing

This is a broad spell focused on emotional healing. Maybe you are healing from a past relationship and your heart chakra is closed. Maybe you had a rough childhood or someone hurt you in some way. Whatever feeling of conflict you have within you—maybe not every moment of the day, but there nonetheless—this spell is meant to help.

I recommend keeping this jar spell in your bedroom, or wherever you let yourself cry. It should be a place of vulnerability.

Many people don't realize it, but the pits of fruit are very powerful. Consider what they are and where they are located: the center of the fruit. If you eat the fruit as well, you are using every part of it for good. I like using sea salt in this spell, as I think the ocean is one of the most magnificent healing wonders on Earth.

Materials

- Geranium
- Dried peach or peach pit
- Sea salt (ethically sourced)
- Bay leaf
- Jar with a cloth to use as a lid
- Writing utensil and paper
- Matches or a lighter
- Blue candle
- Scissors

Place the geranium, dried peach or peach pit, sea salt, and bay leaf into the jar.

Using the writing utensil and paper, write down your intention for emotional healing. Place your paper inside the jar.

Tip: Make it personal. Write to your deities/Spirit/the universe in prayer format.

Light the candle and carefully drip blue candle wax on the contents of the jar, including your intention paper.

When you've finished, blow out or snuff the candle (or let the candle burn out, if you prefer and can do so safely) and make a wish related to the spell's intention.

Leave the lid off the jar, if you're able to do so safely. If this isn't feasible, cut a few 1-inch (2.5 cm) slits in the cloth and tie it on top of the jar.

Keep the jar in your bedroom. Refresh the materials whenever it's necessary.

A Spell for Reducing Fatigue

This is a spell to help reduce general fatigue, which can happen for a lot of reasons. Personally, I often feel fatigue from my anxiety and depression. But you needn't have a health condition to suffer from fatigue from time to time. Low energy is especially common when you are at a difficult time in your life.

If it feels tough to get up the energy to do this spell, take comfort in knowing that the act of doing a spell in and of itself is energetic. Thus, when you focus on increasing energy, it doubles the impact. Don't be afraid to get into the root of your issue in this spell—is it a relationship or your job? The reflection is important. The dispelling is symbolic, but it will feel good, like you are lifting a weight off your chest.

Materials

- Apatite, bloodstone, or citrine

  Note: Universal substitute clear quartz

- Incense stick, elixir or essential oil spray in juniper, lavender, rosemary, mugwort, or mullein, and/or a selenite wand for purifying

- Matches or a lighter

- Orange candle

- Writing utensil and paper

Cleanse the area and the stone with the incense or elixir. You may speak your intentions aloud; for example, "Brighten my space; wash away the decay." Carefully cleanse your aura, too, to purify yourself. If you're using a selenite wand, wave it around your spell space and your aura slowly and intentionally.

Light the candle.

Using the writing utensil and paper, write down what causes your fatigue—for example, a stress-inducing job, a taxing relationship, too much or too little of something (such as social media and sleep, respectively), or a mental/physical health condition.

On another piece of paper, list the ways in which you'll minimize or eliminate your fatigue as best you can—for example, finding a new job, mending a relationship, receiving less or more of something, or seeking out ways to heal.

Hold the stone. Hold the paper on which you listed your fatigue in the flame of the candle and let it burn. (Please do so safely.) Alternatively, you may rip the paper into shreds and dispose of them.

When you've finished, blow out or snuff the candle (or let the candle burn out, if you prefer and can do so safely) and make a wish related to the spell's intention.

Keep the rest of your writing somewhere safe for future reference. Apply your own advice to your life.

A Spell for When You're on Your Period

Do you have difficulties around menstruation? Or maybe just one or two periods per year worse than the rest? No matter, this spell is good for all the pain that can surround a period, whether it is physical or emotional. Use this spell to help get out of the space where you're feeling your worst.

If you have an app or other tracker for your periods, you can also try this spell in the days leading up to it. Do check with your doctor to make sure you can have raspberry leaf tea.

Materials

- Carnelian or blood-stone

  Note: Universal substitute clear quartz

- Incense stick, elixir or essential oil spray in juniper, lavender, rosemary, mugwort, or mullein, and/or a selenite wand

- Matches or a lighter

- Orange candle

- Brewed raspberry leaf tea

Cleanse the area and the stone with the incense or elixir. You may speak your intentions aloud; for example, "Clear this space of that which pains me." Carefully cleanse your aura, too, to purify yourself. If you're using a selenite wand, wave it around your spell space and your aura slowly and intentionally.

Light the candle.

Holding the stone, close your eyes and envision your womb healing.

Pour the tea and drink it.

When you've finished, blow out or snuff the candle (or let the candle burn out, if you prefer and can do so safely) and make a wish related to the spell's intention.

Take some time to practice self-care (read a book, watch a movie, or take a nap or bath).

A Pouch Spell for Spiritual Healing

I consider myself an atheist, but I grew up Catholic. There are still times when I feel chained to or not totally free of my previous religion. Sometimes, I'll see something and think back to my childhood or my fear of confession. Those moments are why I developed this spell.

Healing spiritually could take root for you in a similar way. Maybe it is a previous religion that has left its mark. Or, maybe you feel disconnected from your current deities or they are not responding to you. Have faith. You will find your way again.

Materials

- Labradorite, selenite, or lapis lazuli

  Note: Universal substitute clear quartz

- Incense stick, elixir or essential oil spray, and/ or a selenite wand
- Allspice berries
- Dried blackberries
- Eucalyptus
- Pouch
- Writing utensil and paper
- Twine

Cleanse the area and the stone with the incense or elixir. You may speak your intentions aloud. Carefully cleanse your aura, too, to purify yourself. If you're using a selenite wand, wave it around your spell space and your aura slowly and intentionally.

Place the allspice berries, blackberries, and eucalyptus into the pouch.

Using the writing utensil and paper, write down your intention for spiritual healing. Fold the paper around the stone (you may tie it with twine, if you prefer) and add the bundle to the pouch.

Tip: Make it personal. Write to your deities/Spirit/the universe in prayer format.

Tie the pouch closed and keep it on your altar, or wherever you meditate. Try lying down and placing the pouch on your stomach while meditating, if you like.

A Tea Spell for Physical and Emotional Strength

Turmeric is the golden spice of life, an all-around healing spice. You can use it to help with digestive, brain, joint, and skin health—and the list goes on. If you think it doesn't taste the best, or the flavor is too strong, add some honey to the tea in this spell. Unless you are allergic, I urge you to try it.

Cinnamon is also anti-inflammatory and healing. Use it when you're feeling weak for any reason. Keep in mind that physical and mental issues are often intertwined, one affecting the other. So, it's good to address both.

Materials

- Brewed turmeric or cinnamon tea
- Carnelian or citrine
  Note: Universal substitute clear quartz
- Incense stick or elixir or essential oil spray in juniper, lavender, rosemary, mugwort, or mullein, and/or a selenite wand
- Matches or a lighter
- Orange candle

Pour the tea and drink it throughout the spell.

Cleanse the area and the stone with the incense or elixir. You may speak your intentions aloud; for example, "Purify this space of contaminants, so it may be free of negativity." Carefully cleanse your aura, too, to purify yourself. If you're using a selenite wand, wave it around your spell space and your aura slowly and intentionally.

Light the candle.

Place the stone true south of the candle.

Incant eight times total,

> *"I am strong in body and mind."*

Envision a bright orange light filling your body with strength and vitality.

Continue to drink the tea, focusing on aligning your body and mind as you do so.

When you've finished, blow out or snuff the candle (or let the candle burn out, if you prefer and can do so safely) and make a wish related to the spell's intention.

A Spell for Healing Another's Affliction

It's true that this spell might not do anything beyond putting a smile on a loved one's face—but that is still something. Even if you are gifting it to someone who doesn't believe in witchcraft, they will feel supported. It's a display at the worst, and at the best it will imbue them with extra strength and healing energy. It's like giving flowers, but with healing ingredients. Citrine provides energy and turquoise is healing. The result also smells pleasant, so your recipient can enjoy holding it and inhaling.

Materials

- Citrine or turquoise

  Note: Universal substitute clear quartz

- Incense stick, elixir or essential oil spray, and/or a selenite wand
- Bay leaf
- Chamomile flowers
- Eucalyptus
- Jar with a cloth to use as a lid
- Matches or a lighter
- Green candle
- Writing utensil and paper
- Scissors

Cleanse the area and the stone with the incense or elixir. You may speak your intentions aloud. Carefully cleanse your aura, too, to purify yourself.

Place the bay leaf, chamomile, and eucalyptus into the jar.

Light the candle and carefully drip green candle wax on the herbs.

When you've finished, blow out or snuff the candle (or let the candle burn out, if you prefer and can do so safely) and make a wish related to the spell's intention.

Using the writing utensil and paper, write down your intention to heal another's affliction. Be sure to write their name. Fold the paper around your stone and add the bundle to the jar.

Tip: Make it personal. Write to your deities/Spirit/the universe in prayer format.

Cut a few 1-inch (2.5 cm) slits in the cloth and tie it on top of the jar. Give the jar to the recipient.

A Pouch Spell for Easing the Burden of Grief

If you're dealing with a loss, try this spell. You can also gift it to someone else dealing with loss. The important part is putting thought into the spell. I particularly like rosehips, and Apache tears are supposed to be one of the best remedies for grief. The slip of paper makes it personal. The pouch's portability is key as well, because you will often need it while grieving. There will be times you see something in a public place that reminds you of a person who passed. When you do, you can hold this pouch and pour your emotions into it.

Materials

- Apache tears, amethyst, or lepidolite

  Note: Universal substitute clear quartz

- Incense stick, elixir or essential oil spray, and/or a selenite wand
- Thyme leaves
- Carnation
- Rosehips
- Pouch
- Writing utensil and paper
- Twine

Cleanse the area and the stone with the incense or elixir. You may speak your intentions aloud. Carefully cleanse your aura, too, to purify yourself. If you're using a selenite wand, wave it around your spell space and your aura slowly and intentionally.

Place the thyme, carnation, and rosehips into the pouch, while holding the pouch from the bottom.

Using the writing utensil and paper, write down your intention for healing your grief. Fold the paper around the stone (you may tie it with twine, if you prefer) and add the bundle to the pouch.

Tip: Make it personal. Write to your deities/Spirit/the universe in prayer format.

Tie the pouch closed and keep it in your bedroom when you are not carrying it with you. Whenever you're in the midst of grieving, hold the pouch and feel the full spectrum of your emotions.

ch.6

BANISHING/ BINDING SPELLS

Banishing and binding spells essentially do the same thing, with binding being more intense and potentially less beginner friendly. *Banishing* is mostly about releasing something. *Binding* has more of a trapping effect. So, for example, early in this chapter you'll see spells for banishing things like negativity, which you wouldn't necessarily want to trap—you'd want it away. However, you can also bind negative energy. What's the difference? It's mainly in how you frame it and how you feel.

Let your intuition help you decide whether a banishing spell or a binding spell would be best in any given situation. Maybe you're having nightmares and want to trap something that is causing them. On the other hand, if you feel negative energy in your house or from another person, you may simply wish to banish it or cut ties with that person. To me, it feels more personal and inward, but again there is no right or wrong way to feel about it. Go with what you feel.

A Jar Spell to Trap Negative Energy

Unlike most of the jar spells we've seen so far in this book, this one requires the jar to be lidded. Here's why: This jar will trap negative energy. Typically, this spell is to trap something specific, say if you are in a bad mood in your house quite a bit. This spell is likely more appealing for those who believe in spirits and may not be as appropriate to the secular witch.

Materials

- Smoky quartz

  Note: Universal substitute clear quartz

- Obsidian

  Note: Universal substitute clear quartz

- Incense stick, elixir or essential oil spray, or cleansing bundle

- Jar with a lid

- Knife

- Lemon

- Matches or a lighter

- Black candle wax

Cleanse the area and the stones with the incense, elixir, or cleansing bundle. You may speak your intentions aloud. Carefully cleanse your aura, too, to purify yourself.

Place the smoky quartz and obsidian into the jar.

Using the knife, halve the lemon with one long cut down the middle.

While holding the lemon, incant,

> *"May this fruit absorb the negative entities surrounding me."*

Repeat, incanting six times total.

Place the lemon into the jar. Let it sit uncovered on your altar overnight to attract and trap the negativity.

The next morning, light the candle and seal the lid with black candle wax.

When you've finished, blow out or snuff the candle (or let the candle burn out, if you prefer and can do so safely) and make a wish related to the spell's intention.

Let your intuition guide you as to where you place the jar after sealing it. Dispose the next day, unless you're keeping it in the fridge. As you toss, you may chant something like, "All negativity is trapped. The spell is complete."

A Glass Spell to Trap Negative Energy

Many people believe water holds energy and is one of the most powerful elements you can work with, and smoky quartz is very good at dissolving negativity. I like the idea of using pure filtered water so it has the room to be tainted, or absorb, more of the negative energy. The sea salt is meant to be cleansing and the black pepper is protective. <u>Do not drink this potion!</u>

Materials

- Smoky quartz

  Note: Universal substitute clear quartz

- Incense stick, elixir or essential oil spray, or cleansing bundle
- Drinking glass
- Purified (filtered) water
- Sea salt (ethically sourced)
- Black pepper
- Spoon or other stirring utensil

Cleanse the area and the stone with the incense, elixir, or cleansing bundle. You may speak your intentions aloud. Carefully cleanse your aura, too, to purify yourself.

Place the smoky quartz into the glass.

Fill the glass with water.

Sprinkle in the sea salt and black pepper.

While stirring counterclockwise, incant,

> *"May this potion absorb any and all harmful energy. I remove this energy from my space."*

Repeat the incantation five times, for a total of six times while stirring.

Keep the glass on your altar. Pour the water down the drain when you feel like it has trapped all the bad energy.

A Spell to Banish Stress

Stress, to me, is less of a mental health condition and more circumstantial in nature. For that reason, this spell is meant to be lighter and fresher to help you lighten up a little. You could potentially rename this as a spell to make you happy, as that is my intent! The fresh flowers evoke springtime and new beginnings.

Materials

- Citrine

  Note: Universal substitute clear quartz

- Lily of the valley, orange blossoms, or yellow/orange roses

- Jar with a lid

- Purified (filtered) water

- Spoon or other stirring utensil

Place the citrine and flowers into the jar.

Fill the jar with water.

While stirring counterclockwise, incant,

| *"I am calm; I am at peace."*

Repeat six more times, for a total of seven times.

Cover the jar and let the elixir marinate on your altar for several hours.

Use the elixir in your next bath or shower. Pour it over your body and imagine the stress washing away.

A Spell to Banish Toxic Digital Energy

Our increasingly digital world is convenient and fast, but it brings with it some drawbacks that, while sometimes difficult to notice at first, can get serious. If you've noticed yourself being drawn into your screens more than you want to be, if you've experienced online trolls, scammers, or other negative forces, or if you're concerned about the radiation given off by devices such as cell phones, consider using this spell to banish it all.

Materials

- Smoky quartz

  Note: Universal substitute clear quartz

- Incense stick or elixir or essential oil spray in juniper, lavender, rosemary, or mugwort

- Matches or a lighter

- White candle

- Your mobile phone or other tech device

- Antibacterial wipe

Cleanse the area and the stone with the incense or elixir. You may speak your intentions aloud. Carefully cleanse your aura, too, to purify yourself.

Light the candle.

Wipe down your phone with the antibacterial wipe.

Incant ten times total,

> *"I pray for the higher evolvement of digital negativity. Transform, transform, transform."*

Place the smoky quartz on your phone for a few hours. Do not leave the candle unattended.

When you've finished, blow out or snuff the candle (or let the candle burn out, if you prefer and can do so safely) and make a wish related to the spell's intention.

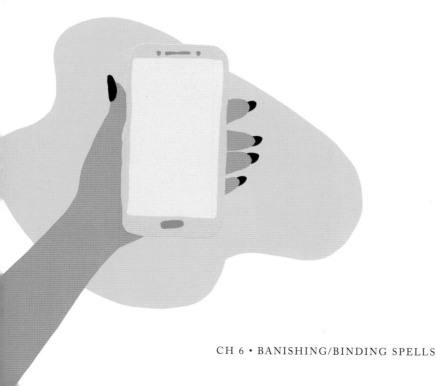

A Jar Spell to Drive Away a Hostile Presence or Bad Energy

Similar to A Glass Spell to Trap Negative Energy (page 109), this is a spell for those who have run into a feeling of something or some presence bringing them down. If you're spiritual, you might think you are being haunted, but there are other ways to receive this feeling. You don't need to believe a ghost is trailing you to use this spell. Stale or gloomy energy is reason enough.

Materials

- Table salt
- Bay leaves
- Whole cloves
- Basil
- Jar with a cloth to use as a lid
- Writing utensil and paper
- Matches or a lighter
- Black candle
- Scissors

Place the salt, bay leaves, cloves, and basil into the jar.

Using the writing utensil and paper, write a short letter forbidding negative spirits from entering your home and add the letter to the jar.

Light the candle and carefully drip black candle wax atop the contents of the jar.

When you've finished, blow out or snuff the candle (or let the candle burn out, if you prefer and can do so safely) and make a wish related to the spell's intention.

Place the jar near your front door. Leave the lid off the jar, if you are able to do so safely, so it may work as a sort of vacuum. If this isn't feasible, cut several 1-inch (2.5 cm) slits in the cloth and tie it on top of the jar. Leave the jar out as long as the ingredients stay fresh. Dispose when you feel it's complete.

A Spell to Release Toxic Thought Patterns

This spell is wonderful for releasing the negative thoughts you frequently experience—the ones that might be manifesting as false perceptions of yourself, others, or your environment. Consider doing this spell before A Spell to Banish a Bad Habit (page 116). For example, if you are down on yourself for not quitting a relationship that is not good for you, you might be getting down on yourself for being "too much." That thought, which opposes self-love, is toxic and must be broken.

Note: Sometimes, you have to search for the toxic thoughts that lurk underneath bad habits. Finding and eliminating a toxic subconscious thought pattern can be surprisingly powerful.

Materials

- Black tourmaline

  Note: Universal substitute clear quartz

- Incense stick or elixir or essential oil spray in juniper, lavender, rosemary, mugwort, or mullein

- Matches or a lighter

- White candle

- Cast-iron cauldron or pot

- Writing utensil and paper

Cleanse the area and stone with the incense or elixir. You may speak your intentions aloud. Carefully cleanse your aura, too, to purify yourself.

Light the candle and place it in the cauldron.

Using the writing utensil and paper, write down negative thoughts you're currently experiencing or frequently encounter.

Carefully burn the paper in the cauldron.

Holding the black tourmaline, incant eight times total,

> *"I liberate myself from negative thinking."*

When you've finished, blow out or snuff the candle (or let the candle burn out, if you prefer and can do so safely) and make a wish related to the spell's intention.

Cleanse the area again with the incense or elixir to remove any lingering toxicity.

A Spell to Banish a Bad Habit

Maybe it's as small as biting your nails or maybe it's as dangerous as smoking cigarettes, but bad habits can be hard to break. A bad habit may also be something less obvious, like a romantic partner who is not good to you, but you can't seem to "quit" them. This spell is good for all of these reasons and more.

Materials

- Writing utensil and paper
- Table salt or black salt
- Cast-iron cauldron or pot
- Black candle
- Matches or a lighter

Using the writing utensil and paper, write down the bad habit you wish to banish.

Sprinkle a salt circle around the cauldron and candle.

Light the candle and place it inside the cauldron.

Carefully burn the paper in the cauldron and, as you do so, incant the following eight times total,

> *"Bad habit, I banish thee,*
> *get lost and never return to me."*

When you've finished, blow out or snuff the candle (or let the candle burn out, if you prefer and can do so safely) and make a wish related to the spell's intention.

The next day, clean out your cauldron and have gratitude as you do so for being one step closer to breaking that bad habit. You may bury the ashes or scatter them.

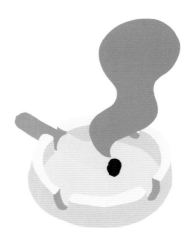

A Super Simple Binding Spell

I love this spell because it is so easy. It's a lot like A Jar Spell to Trap Negative Energy (page 108) in effect, but quicker to perform. This spell is a sort of metaphor for binding, in general, which can freeze something bad coming for you. Note that when you dispose of the lemon, you should not think of whatever you were binding thawing and coming back for you. The intention behind the spell remains, but if you want to close the spell while focusing your intention, you can incant something as you dispose of it.

Materials

- Writing utensil and small piece of paper
- Knife
- Lemon
- Twine

Using the writing utensil and paper, write down that which you wish to bind. This may be a person or thing causing harm or strife in your life.

Use the knife to cut open the lemon, starting at the stem, but not cutting the lemon in half fully.

Stuff the paper into the lemon. Wrap the lemon with twine and tie it closed.

Place the lemon in your freezer for 48 hours.

Bury the lemon, or simply dispose of it. As you do so, thank deity/Spirit/universe you choose to work with for aiding you.

A Pouch Spell to Bind Negativity

The reason I love this spell to bind negativity is because of its portability. Maybe you're traveling and need this sort of help while out and about. If you're an empath, you may be especially sensitive, and this spell can help on your daily journeys out and about. However, even if you are generally tough, it can also be good for gatherings with deep grief and sadness, such as a funeral.

Materials

- Dried thyme leaves
- Pouch
- Writing utensil and small piece of paper
- Knife
- Lime
- Twine
- Vinegar

Place the thyme into the pouch.

Using the writing utensil and paper, write down that which you wish to bind.

Use the knife to cut open the lime, starting at the stem, but not cutting the lime in half fully.

Stuff the paper into the lime. Wrap the lime with twine, tie it closed, and add it to the pouch.

Sprinkle the contents of the pouch with vinegar.

Bring the pouch with you while you travel. When you return, if you choose, place the pouch on your altar. When the contents of the pouch begin to rot, thank deity/Spirit/universe and dispose of it (i.e., throw away the contents and wash the pouch so you can reuse it).

ch.7

SLEEP AND RELAXATION SPELLS

The number one thing to know here is that a well-rested witch is a witch who succeeds. If you're really tired, it's going to be harder to calm your mind and manifest in the way you want. Not to mention all the other downsides of being tired, whether your work suffers, or you are too tired to enjoy time with family. I consider many of the spells in this chapter essential because, if you're not well rested, your other spells will simply be less effective. Get the rest you need to function optimally.

Related: Never apologize for taking a break when you need one. Listen and respond to your body and psyche; slow down and rest until you feel well again. As a witch, you must take the time to care for yourself in order to effect significant change through your craft. A worn-out witch is like a laptop on low battery; you won't perform the way you would with juice. Recharge without shame.

WITCHY TIP: DRINK CALMING TEA BEFORE BED

As a hardworking witch, you need rest to work your magick effectively, so prioritize it! Make a habit of winding down with calming tea every evening, about an hour before bedtime. Stir your tea clockwise and incant six times, "I will sleep well."

A Candle Spell for Sleep

This spell is simple and straightforward. It is only three steps and requires only three items. Maybe you have a big day tomorrow and want to go to bed early. Devote just a few moments to this spell and then try to get the rest you need. This spell is best performed one hour before bedtime.

Materials

- White or purple candle
- Lavender essential oil
- Matches or a lighter

Anoint the candle with lavender essential oil by rubbing the oil on the candle (this is also called dressing a candle). Light the candle.

Note: With any essential oil you should dilute the oil before handling and do a patch test on your skin to test for a negative reaction.

Cup your hands a safe distance over the flame and softly incant seven times total,

> *"Spirit, help me sleep tonight—*
> *may my body rest and my dreams delight."*

Leave the candle burning, as long as you're awake. Do not leave the candle unattended. Before you go to sleep, blow out or snuff the candle (or let the candle burn out, if you prefer and can do so safely) and make a wish related to the spell's intention.

WITCHY TIP: FOR INSOMNIACS

Can't sleep? Brew chamomile or jasmine tea. Add a nut- or plant-based milk. Using a spoon, stir clockwise and incant twice,

> *"Sleep, sleep, come to me, may I rest in peaceful harmony."*

Sip the tea slowly with your eyes closed. Loosen the muscles in your body, starting from your toes and moving upward.

A Jar Spell for Restful Sleep

This is a more intense version of A Candle Spell for Sleep (page 123). Maybe you don't just have a big day tomorrow, but a big week ahead. I think it's a great spell for Sunday to set the tone for the week ahead. The aroma is a big part of this spell: Enjoy the anise, jasmine, and peppermint.

Materials

- Aniseed
- Jasmine flowers
- Peppermint leaves
- Jar with a cloth to use as a lid
- Writing utensil and paper
- Lavender essential oil
- Scissors
- Twine (optional)

Place the aniseed, jasmine flowers, and peppermint leaves into the jar.

Using the writing utensil and paper, write down your intention to have restful sleep. Add the paper to the jar.

Drip about 4 drops of lavender essential oil on the contents of the jar.

Leave the lid off the jar, if you're able to do so safely. If this isn't feasible, cut several 1-inch (2.5 cm) slits in the cloth and tie it on top of the jar.

When you can't sleep, breathe in the fragrance from the jar. Relax every muscle in your body. Leave the jar on your nightstand and refresh the ingredients whenever it's necessary.

WITCHY TIP: SWEET SLEEPY-TIME ELIXIR

Here's a witchy dessert elixir to whip up an hour or two before bedtime: In a saucepan over low heat, slowly warm 1 cup (240 ml) or less of oat milk or almond milk and add a few squares of white chocolate. (Important: Make sure the chocolate contains no caffeine.) Stir and warm until the chocolate dissolves. Stir in several sprigs of fresh lavender and cover the pan for a couple of minutes, just until the elixir begins to steam. Turn off the heat and remove the pan from the burner. Let sit for just a moment longer, then pour the elixir into a mug (straining out the lavender). Add a dollop of almond butter. Stir and enjoy!

A Pouch Spell to Expel Nightmares

Waking up from a night of disturbing dreams can be exhausting and anxiety-inducing. In order to cleanse, take a warm sea salt bath right away, or shower with sea salt–infused soap. To avoid future nightmares, keep this pouch spell by your bedside.

Materials

- Moonstone

  Note: Universal substitute clear quartz

- Incense stick or elixir or essential oil spray in juniper, lavender, rosemary, mugwort, or mullein

- Dandelion root
- Jasmine flowers
- Thyme leaves
- Peppermint leaves
- Sachet or cloth bag

Cleanse the area and stone with the incense or elixir. You may speak your intentions aloud. Carefully cleanse your aura, too, to purify yourself.

Place the moonstone, dandelion root, jasmine flowers, thyme, and peppermint into the sachet.

Hold the bag. Visualize a bright lavender light zapping away your nightmares.

Keep the bag on your nightstand. Refresh the ingredients whenever it's necessary.

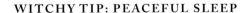

WITCHY TIP: PEACEFUL SLEEP

Keep selenite and lepidolite crystals on a windowsill in your bedroom. Pray over the stones once a week; ask your deities/Spirit/the universe for tranquil slumber and sweet dreams.

A Spell to Summon Clairvoyant Dreams

*Who doesn't want a psychic dream? If you are unfamiliar with the term, **clairvoyant** means "clear seeing." So, a clairvoyant dream is along those lines: a divine image that comes to you. Whether you want to see something specific or are just trying to hone your psychic side, this spell is a good place to start. You must stay patient, though, as I can almost guarantee this spell will not produce results the first time you cast it. It may take weeks or months to work. Or, it may work and then you forget most of, or all of, the dream. You may even find that this is not for you. That's okay, too.*

Materials

- Moonstone or labradorite

  Note: Universal substitute clear quartz

- Incense stick or elixir or essential oil spray in juniper, lavender, rosemary, mugwort, or mullein

- Third-eye chakra meditation music (available on YouTube)

- Writing utensil and paper

Before bedtime, cleanse your sleeping area and the stone with the incense or elixir. You may speak your intentions aloud. Carefully cleanse your aura, too, to purify yourself.

Turn on the meditation music, which will play through the night.

Using the writing utensil and paper, write down, in detail, what or whom you wish to see and/or questions you're seeking answers to. You may draw symbols or pictures that resonate with your psychic abilities.

Fold the paper into a small square and tuck it beneath your pillow. Keep the stone near your bed.

When you wake up, quickly record your findings.

A Sea-Themed Jar Spell to Promote Inner Peace

I see this as a fun summer spell. If you are a beach person or love jumping into the water any time you get the chance, this spell may be for you. (Or, maybe you just have a lot of water signs in your chart!) I feel it sweeps you away and gives you the peaceful visual of being on the beach. It may not be the thriftiest spell due to the bergamot essential oil, but you can substitute lime.

Materials

- Larimar, blue calcite, or blue kyanite

  Note: Universal substitute clear quartz

- Incense stick, elixir or essential oil spray, or cleansing bundle
- Beach sand
- Dried coconut
- Sea salt (ethically sourced)
- Jar
- Bergamot essential oil
- Spoon or other stirring utensil

Cleanse the area and the stone with the incense, elixir, or cleansing bundle. You may speak your intentions aloud. Carefully cleanse your aura, too, to purify yourself.

Place the beach sand, dried coconut, and sea salt into the jar.

Add 5 or so drops of bergamot essential oil to the jar. Stir the contents clockwise.

Add the stone. Leave the jar unlidded.

Keep the jar in your bedroom to promote inner peace. You may also meditate while holding it.

A Potion Spell for Combatting Nightmares

If you're struggling with nightmares or wake up with a pit in your stomach, this is a good spell for easing that. I find this spell is also helpful if you're battling anxiety that is causing bad or uncomfortable dreams. Remember: Water holds energy. In this spell, picture the water sucking up any negative energy from your psyche.

Materials

- Amethyst

  Note: Universal substitute clear quartz

- Incense, elixir or essential oil spray, or cleansing bundle

- Drinking glass

- Purified (filtered) water

- Sea salt (ethically sourced)

- Spoon or other stirring utensil

Cleanse the area and the stone with the incense, elixir, or cleansing bundle. You may speak your intentions aloud. Carefully cleanse your aura, too, to purify yourself.

Place the amethyst into the glass.

Pour the purified water over the stone.

Sprinkle in sea salt.

Stirring clockwise, incant a total of seven times:

| *"May I have sweet dreams tonight and every night."*

Keep on your nightstand or near your bed. Refresh every evening.

A Pouch Spell for Pleasant Dreams

Perhaps you're on a trip or sleeping in a strange place. It's safe to say most people don't sleep as well when not sleeping in their own bed. This spell could help, at least a little. I've found this pouch will stay at its best for about a week before it needs to be refreshed.

Materials

- Lepidolite or moonstone
  Note: Universal substitute clear quartz
- Incense stick, elixir or essential oil spray, or cleansing bundle
- Bay laurel
- Chamomile flowers
- Fresh lavender flowers or lavender essential oil
- Pouch
- Writing utensil and paper
- Twine

Cleanse the area and the stone with the incense, elixir, or cleansing bundle. You may speak your intentions aloud. Carefully cleanse your aura, too, to purify yourself.

Place the bay laurel, chamomile, and lavender into the pouch. (If you're using lavender essential oil, sprinkle a few drops on the chamomile and bay laurel, or rub the leaves with it.)

Using the writing utensil and paper, write down your intention to have sweet dreams. Fold the paper around the crystal (you may tie it with twine, if you prefer) and add the bundle to the pouch.

Tip: Make it personal. Write to your deities/Spirit/the universe in prayer format.

Tie the pouch closed. Keep it on your nightstand or under your pillow. Open the pouch and take a deep breath before bedtime. Remember to re-tie the pouch before falling asleep.

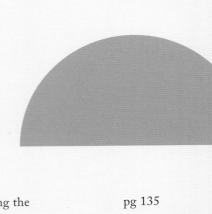

ch.8

PSYCHIC SPELLS

This chapter is last because it addresses a more advanced aspect of witchcraft. Yet, there's nothing to be afraid of. You do not need to know everything before you start, and you don't need to be perfect at your craft to explore your psychic gifts.

I feel like a lot of witches can relate to this: Maybe you had strong intuition about things you can't explain as a kid. For example, I realized I was a witch shortly after an intense meditation session with my family psychic. A few days later, I was driving in my neighborhood at night when I suddenly knew that an animal was going to cross the road in front of me. I slowed my car and, sure enough, a bunny hopped out into the road. If you also have these uncanny predictions, this chapter might appeal to you.

That said, if you have never had these feelings, there is nothing wrong with that. Looking into clairvoyance, receiving a vision of something happening, is simply interesting. If you identify as a witch, you have the ability to tap into these gifts. You just have to know they are there and trust yourself deeply. Know that you have witchy intuition deep down and you just have to unearth it.

WITCHY TIP: DIVINATION

Pay attention to which form of divination calls to you as you cast these spells. I highly recommend trying something such as tarot cards or a pendulum after you cast the first two spells in this chapter and establish your presence.

A Spell for Entering the Spiritual Gateway

This is a great first spell for the chapter as it's meant to be a general entry to the spiritual realm. It can be a lifelong journey to understand and hone your psychic skills, but it all begins by opening your mind to start communicating with the universe. Most of us, especially those of us who aren't that spiritual, have to start from ground zero. We have to open ourselves to the concept of this new way of communicating before asking questions or doing a reading.

Materials

- Amethyst

  Note: Universal substitute clear quartz

- Incense stick, elixir or essential oil spray in juniper, lavender, rosemary, mugwort, or mullein, and/or a selenite wand

- Matches or a lighter

- Blue candle

- Music in 852 Hz (available on YouTube; visit meditativemind.org/ cleanse-your-mind-with-852hz-solfeggio-frequency-music/ for more information.)

- Speakers or headphones (optional)

Note: For this spell, you may sit or stand; position yourself however you feel most comfortable and empowered.

Cleanse the area and the stone with the incense or elixir. You may speak your intentions aloud; for example, "Clear the air; refine for the divine." Carefully cleanse your aura, too, to purify yourself. If you're using a selenite wand, wave it around your spell space and your aura slowly and intentionally.

Light the candle.

Play the music in 852 Hz. Use speakers or headphones for an amplified effect.

Bask in the music for a minute or two; practice deep breathing. Continue playing the music until the end of the spell.

Place your hands in prayer form, with the amethyst stone in the middle of your palms. Incant,

> *"Divine, divine,*
> *open my mind.*
>
> *Spirit, spirit,*
> *I do not fear it."*

Recite this a total of eleven times.

Close your eyes. Visualize a heavenly gate opening, inviting you in. Walk through it. Revel in the joy of the place you've taken on the spiritual plane.

When you've finished, blow out or snuff the candle (or let the candle burn out, if you prefer and can do so safely) and make a wish related to the spell's intention.

A Spell for Psychic Protection and Introductory Communication

This spell is comprehensive, but not difficult. We are taking steps to explore our communication with another realm, but this spell touches on the importance of protecting yourself as you do so. I am not particularly superstitious, but many others are. There is nothing wrong with attention to safety if it makes you feel more comfortable.

Materials

- Amethyst, black tourmaline, or hematite

  Note: Universal substitute clear quartz

- Incense stick, elixir or essential oil spray in juniper, lavender, rosemary, mugwort, or mullein, and/or a selenite wand

- Matches or a lighter

- Black candle

- Music in 417 Hz (available on YouTube; visit mindfulnessexercises. com/417-hz-wipes-negative-energy/ for more information.)

- Speakers or headphones (optional)

Note: For this spell, you may sit or stand; position yourself however you feel most comfortable and empowered.

Cleanse the area and the stone with the incense or elixir. You may speak your intentions aloud; for example, "Eliminate that which may harm me." Carefully cleanse your aura, too, to purify yourself. If you're using a selenite wand, wave it around your spell space and your aura slowly and intentionally.

Light the candle.

Play the music in 417 Hz. Use speakers or headphones for an amplified effect.

Bask in the music for a few minutes. As you do so, envision yourself casting a circle. Imagine a white, purple, or blue light rushing out of your aura and into the surrounding area. The light will take shape as a sphere that encompasses you, the stone, and the candle completely. Incant one time total,

> *"My circle is cast; within it, I am safe on my journey to the spirit world."*

Continue playing the music until the end of the spell. Talk to whatever entity you feel drawn to. Some people say Spirit, for the all-encompassing divine. But you may feel drawn to a certain god or goddess, or even a loved one who has passed. Don't ask for anything—would you ask someone you just met, or met for the first time in a new way, for a favor? Instead, focus on cultivating a positive and mutually beneficial relationship.

When you're finished, envision the light of the circle shrinking into your core. Say,

| *"Thank you, Spirit. The circle is now closed."*

When you've finished, blow out or snuff the candle (or let the candle burn out, if you prefer and can do so safely) and make a wish related to the spell's intention.

A Pouch Spell for Heightened Intuition

Before we get into heavier rituals or practices in the spirit world, I strongly encourage you to uncover and trust your intuition. I think witches have a special form of intuition. You've realized you're unique in some way and are more in touch than the average person with what's going on in the world around you— and beyond you. It's important to carry this spell around as often as you can, as you begin to work on the other spells in this chapter. It represents that you're on a journey to opening and harnessing the power of your psychic gifts. It's crucial you get to a place where you trust your gut.

Materials

- Labradorite or sodalite
  Note: Universal substitute clear quartz
- Incense stick, elixir or essential oil spray, or cleansing bundle
- Bay leaf
- Star anise
- Lemon balm leaves or lemongrass essential oil
- Pouch
- Writing utensil and paper
- Twine

Cleanse the area and the stone with the incense, elixir, or cleansing bundle. You may speak your intentions aloud. Carefully cleanse your aura, too, to purify yourself.

Place the bay leaf, star anise, and lemon balm into the pouch. (If you're using essential oil, sprinkle it on the ingredients or rub it onto the bay leaf.)

Using the writing utensil and paper, write down your intention to connect with your intuition. Fold the paper around your crystal (you may tie it with twine, if you prefer) and add the bundle to the pouch.

Tip: Make it personal. Write to your deities/Spirit/the universe in prayer format.

Tie the pouch closed and keep it on your altar, or wherever you meditate. Open the pouch before practicing divination. Re-tie it once you've finished your session.

A Jar Spell to Increase Your Psychic Abilities

Like other jar spells in this book, the spell itself is easy, but can have lasting effects over time. This spell is especially fitting in this chapter because the goal with all the spells is less about instant results and more about developing a relationship and changing the way you think about your place in the universe. Cinnamon represents strength and power, and yarrow and celery are good at promoting psychic opening (yarrow also helps banish negativity). Celery seed can also help with focus—if you have too much clutter in your mind working against you.

Materials

- Amethyst
  Note: Universal substitute clear quartz
- Incense stick, elixir or essential oil spray, or cleansing bundle
- Celery seed
- Cinnamon sticks or ground cinnamon
- Yarrow flowers
- Jar with a cloth to use as a lid
- Writing utensil and paper
- Scissors

Cleanse the area and the stone with the incense, elixir, or cleansing bundle. You may speak your intentions aloud. Carefully cleanse your aura, too, to purify yourself.

Place the celery seed, cinnamon, and yarrow flowers into the jar.

Using the writing utensil and paper, write down your intention to understand and tap into your psychic abilities. Fold the paper around the amethyst and add the bundle to the jar.

Tip: Make it personal. Write to your deities/Spirit/the universe in prayer format.

Leave the lid off the jar, if you're able to do so safely. If this isn't feasible, cut a few 1-inch (2.5 cm) slits in the cloth and tie it on top of the jar.

Keep the jar on your altar, or wherever you meditate. Look at the jar from time to time and meditate on it for 5 to 15 minutes.

If you want to take this spell a step further, you can even hold the jar, close your eyes, and imagine yourself floating through space to the spirit world. Introduce yourself to any beings that may be there. It should be a calming exercise. When you are ready to leave, travel back and make sure you are firmly back in your body.

Note: If at any time you feel uncomfortable, just picture yourself back in the present moment and open your eyes.

Dispose whenever you feel the spell is complete. You may thank Spirit, the universe, or your deities as you do so.

A Spell for Clairvoyance (Clear Seeing)

Clairvoyance is also known as clear seeing. It could be a symbol in your head or a graphic visual. There is a form of visualization called scrying, an energetic reading of sorts, where you look at a reflective surface and wait for an image to appear. (I did this once for two hours and nothing happened. I gave up in frustration, and that's okay! I am drawn to claircognizance.) That's an intense version of clairvoyance. Dreams are probably the easiest way to experience clairvoyance. My advice is to take it easy and see if clairvoyance is for you.

Materials

- Labradorite, moonstone, or lapis lazuli

  Note: Universal substitute clear quartz

- Incense stick, elixir or essential oil spray in juniper, lavender, rosemary, mugwort, or mullein, and/or a selenite wand

- Matches or a lighter

- White candle

- Writing utensil and paper

Note: For this spell, you may sit or stand; position yourself however you feel most comfortable and empowered.

Cleanse the area and the stone with the incense or elixir. You may speak your intentions aloud; for example, "Draw away that which obstructs my view." Carefully cleanse your aura, too, to purify yourself. If you're using a selenite wand, wave it around your spell space and your aura slowly and intentionally.

Light the candle.

Breathe deeply for a few minutes. As you do so, envision your third eye opening.

Using the writing utensil and paper, draw an open eye on the paper. When you're finished, place the stone on the eye.

Incant seven times total,

> *"I have no fear, my vision is clear."*

When you've finished, blow out or snuff the candle (or let the candle burn out, if you prefer and can do so safely) and make a wish related to the spell's intention.

WITCHY TIP: CLAIRVOYANCE

Another option to experience clairvoyance is to light a few candles, meditate, and draw. Don't look at your hands while drawing. When finished, look at the image and see if you can make sense of it.

A Spell for Claircognizance (Clear Knowing)

Claircognizance is also known as clear knowing. This is my favorite of the "clairs" because it came most naturally to me and because I have enjoyed exploring it. In fact, I just naturally found myself coming back to this form of psychic ability and I suspect you will find one of the three clairs in this section of spells resonates more strongly with you than the others. Don't be afraid to follow your witchy intuition and spend the most time with the form of communication you like most.

Materials

- Amethyst, turquoise, or fluorite

  Note: Universal substitute clear quartz

- Incense stick, elixir or essential oil spray in juniper, lavender, rosemary, mugwort, or mullein, and/or a selenite wand

- Matches or a lighter

- White candle

- Writing utensil and paper

Note: For this spell, you may sit or stand; position yourself however you feel most comfortable and empowered.

Cleanse the area and the stone with the incense or elixir. You may speak your intentions aloud; for example, "Eliminate clutter that blocks my knowing." Carefully cleanse your aura, too, to purify yourself. If you're using a selenite wand, wave it around your spell space and your aura slowly and intentionally.

Light the candle.

Breathe deeply for a few minutes. As you do so, imagine your mind is healthy and sharp.

Using the writing utensil and paper, draw a brain on the paper. When you're finished, place the stone on the brain.

Incant,

| *"I have no fear, my knowledge is clear."*

Repeat this seven more times, for a total of eight times.

When you've finished, blow out or snuff the candle (or let the candle burn out, if you prefer and can do so safely) and make a wish related to the spell's intention.

A Spell for Clairaudience (Clear Hearing)

Clairaudience is also known as clear hearing. This can be a little tough to describe, but if you listen with regularity to podcasts or audiobooks and find you absorbed the information really well, you likely may possess this skill. Or, if in school you were an auditory learner, you may be more adept at clairaudience. That said, don't expect literal voices. It is not a hallucination but, rather, more like someone speaking to you in a dream. You will recognize the difference between someone whispering in your ear and experiencing an auditory message delivered by the spirit realm.

Materials

- Selenite, angelite, or chrysocolla

  Note: Universal substitute clear quartz

- Incense stick, elixir or essential oil spray in juniper, lavender, rosemary, mugwort, or mullein, and/or a selenite wand

- Matches or a lighter

- White candle

- Writing utensil and paper

Note: For this spell, you may sit or stand; position yourself however you feel most comfortable and empowered.

Cleanse the area and the stone with the incense or elixir. You may speak your intentions aloud; for example, "Remove that which impedes my hearing." Carefully cleanse your aura, too, to purify yourself. If you're using a selenite wand, wave it around your spell space and your aura slowly and intentionally.

Light the candle.

Breathe deeply for a few minutes. As you do so, imagine that your ears are healthy and sharp.

Using the writing utensil and paper, draw two ears on the paper. When you're finished, place the stone on the ears.

Incant,

> *"I have no fear; I hear loud and clear."*

Repeat this seven more times, for a total of eight times.

When you've finished, blow out or snuff the candle (or let the candle burn out, if you prefer and can do so safely) and make a wish related to the spell's intention.

A Potion Spell for Psychic Wisdom

This is a super simple but very cool spell. The energy from the stone and the water enters your body. Drink this potion first thing in the morning if you're going to cast a lot of spells that day. And, if you have a lot of water symbols in your chart, it will be extra appealing.

Materials

- Medium-large amethyst

  Note: Universal substitute clear quartz

- Incense stick, elixir or essential oil spray, or cleansing bundle

- Drinking glass

- Purified (filtered) water

- Eco-friendly straw (such as bamboo or metal)

Cleanse the area and the stone with the incense, elixir, or cleansing bundle. You may speak your intentions aloud. Carefully cleanse your aura, too, to purify yourself.

Place the amethyst into the glass.

Fill the glass with water.

Hold the glass and pray your intention. Visualize a purple light energizing your psychic abilities.

Put the potion in your fridge for 10 minutes.

Incant seven times total,

| *"I am awake; activate my psychic center."*

Drink the potion in its entirety using your straw so you don't choke. Drink slowly and intentionally. Remove the amethyst from the glass and place it on your altar. Leave it there as long as it feels right.

A Spell to Prepare for Spiritual Dreams

What is a spiritual dream? To me, it is the type of dream after which you wake up and know it's important. You want to run and write down the dream immediately, even if it's the middle of the night. (Note: Take it from me, write it down! You will forget it by morning if you wake up in the middle of the night.) You can even do a voice memo instead of writing, if that's easier. This spell is best performed just before bedtime, or even an hour or two before you go to bed. It will probably make you sleepy.

Materials

- Moonstone and labradorite, sodalite, and/or chrysocolla

  Note: Universal substitute clear quartz

- Incense stick, elixir or essential oil spray in juniper, lavender, rosemary, mugwort, or mullein, and/or a selenite wand

- Matches or a lighter

- Purple candle

- Music in 528 Hz (available on YouTube; visit mindfulnessexercises. com/528hz-miracle-tone/ for more information.)

- Speakers or headphones (optional)

- Writing utensil and paper

- Frankincense and/or lavender essential oil

- Sleep meditation music (available on YouTube; optional)

Note: For this spell, you may sit or stand; position yourself however you feel most comfortable and empowered.

Cleanse the area and the stone(s) with the incense or elixir. You may speak your intentions aloud; for example, "Remove all blockages; open my line to Spirit." Carefully cleanse your aura, too, to purify yourself. If you're using a selenite wand, wave it around your spell space and your aura slowly and intentionally.

Light the candle.

Play the music in 528 Hz. Use speakers or headphones for an amplified effect.

Bask in the music for a minute or two. Practice deep breathing and "ohm-ing" to the music. Continue playing the music until the end of the spell.

Place the stone(s) in your palms and hold them over your heart. Incant,

> *"Divine—*
> *open my eye as I lie asleep,*
> *into Spirit's realm, escort me deep.*
>
> *Send me a message, symbol, or sign;*
> *speak to me clearly, as one we intertwine."*

Recite the incantation ten more times, for a total of eleven times.

Using the writing utensil and paper, write down the incantation. Dowse it with essential oil and place the paper under your pillow before going to sleep.

When you've finished, blow out or snuff the candle (or let the candle burn out, if you prefer and can do so safely) and make a wish related to the spell's intention.

Optional: Play sleep meditation music while you sleep and keep your stones near or on your bed.

A Spell to Open Your Third Eye

This spell is toward the end of the chapter because it's more complex than simply starting your intuition, and it gets into chakra work—which you may or may not feel drawn to. The third eye is the chakra for your psychic gifts, but you don't need to be an expert in chakra work. It's the chakra located between your eyebrows and it's responsible for psychic wisdom. This spell is especially for people whose third-eye chakra is blocked. (You can take quizzes online to determine if your chakra is blocked.)

Materials

- Amethyst

  Note: Universal substitute clear quartz

- Incense stick, elixir or essential oil spray in juniper, lavender, rosemary, mugwort, or mullein, and/or a selenite wand

- Sandalwood, lavender, or rosemary essential oil, diluted in a carrier oil (important: do a patch test before the spell to test for any negative reaction)

- Matches or a lighter

- Purple candle

Note: For this spell, you may sit or stand; position yourself however you feel most comfortable.

Cleanse the area and the stone with the incense or elixir. You may speak your intentions aloud; for example, "Remove that which blocks or hinders." Carefully cleanse your aura, too, to purify yourself. If you're using a selenite wand, wave it around your spell space and your aura slowly and intentionally.

Place 3 drops of diluted sandalwood essential oil on your wrists and temples.

Light the candle. Cup your hands a safe distance away from the flame. Feel the warmth radiating through your body. Close your eyes and take a few deep breaths.

Hold the amethyst over your third eye (centered between your eyebrows, above your nose).

Chant,

> *"My wisdom flows from within; I remain in touch with my truth.*
>
> *I am a constant point of insight. My intuition emanates eternally."*

Close your eyes and visualize your third eye opening. Hum or sing as you do so, if you wish.

When you've finished, blow out or snuff the candle (or let the candle burn out, if you prefer and can do so safely) and make a wish related to the spell's intention.

A Spell to Revive Your Psychic Skills

This is the spell for when you feel you've lost touch with your gifts. We all get busy sometimes and it's possible to fall out of practice. Your gifts are not lost. They are just buried beneath the clutter of your everyday life. This is a spell to unearth those abilities and get them back top of mind.

Materials

- Labradorite, selenite, or lapis lazuli

  Note: Universal substitute clear quartz

- Incense stick, elixir or essential oil spray, or cleansing bundle

- Brewed cinnamon or bay leaf tea

- Matches or a lighter

- Silver or white candle

Cleanse the area and the stone with the incense, elixir, or cleansing bundle. You may speak your intentions aloud. Carefully cleanse your aura, too, to purify yourself.

Pour and sip the tea throughout the spell.

Light the candle.

Place the stone between your palms in prayer position.

Incant the following seven times total,

> *"[Deity/Spirit/universe], imbue me with your wisdom;*
> *I request access to all records—*
> *from now and forevermore.*
> *I thank you; blessings."*

When you've finished, blow out or snuff the candle (or let the candle burn out, if you prefer and can do so safely) and make a wish related to the spell's intention.

A Tea Spell for Spiritual Insight

This is another spell where you'll literally drink the energy. It's another form of receiving a message and my advice is to try every way you can! One spell form may work better for you than another. In this spell, we're combining the power of herbs with fire magic. Don't expect something to happen right away, though. I like this spell just before bedtime.

Materials

- Matches or a lighter
- Indigo or purple candle
- Brewed marshmallow root or lemon balm tea

Light the candle.

Pour the tea and hold your hands above it.

While focusing on the candle flame, incant the following five times total,

> *"I am open to divine information. [Deity/Spirit/universe], grant me wisdom."*

Drink the tea at your leisure.

When you've finished, blow out or snuff the candle (or let the candle burn out, if you prefer and can do so safely) and make a wish related to the spell's intention.

Resources

Books

Encyclopedia of Crystals, Revised and Expanded
by Judy Hall

Psychic Witch:
A Metaphysical Guide to Meditation, Magick, and Manifestation
by Mat Auryn

The Green Witch: Your Complete Guide to the Natural Magic of Herbs, Flowers, Essential Oils, and More
by Arin Murphy-Hiscock

The Modern Witchcraft Guide to Magickal Herbs:
Your Complete Guide to the Hidden Powers of Herbs
by Judy Ann Nock

The Ultimate Guide to Divination: The Beginner's Guide to Using Cards, Crystals, Runes, Palmistry, and More for Insight and Predicting the Future
by Liz Dean

The Witch's Book of Self-Care:
Magical Ways to Pamper, Soothe, and Care for Your Body and Spirit
by Arin Murphy-Hiscock

Waking the Witch:
Reflections on Women, Magic, and Power
by Pam Grossman

Witchery: Embrace the Witch Within
by Juliet Diaz

Websites Referenced and Educational Sites

www.astro.cafeastrology.com

www.badwitch.es

www.chakras.info

www.charmsoflight.com

www.chestnutherbs.com

www.color-meanings.com

www.debrasilvermanastrology.com

www.energymuse.com

www.learnreligions.com

www.lunalunamagazine.com

www.mindbodygreen.com

www.moongiant.com

www.plentifulearth.com

www.theherbalacademy.com

www.thehoodwitch.com

www.thetravelingwitch.com

www.wiccaliving.com

www.wicca-spirituality.com

www.witchipedia.com

Herbs, Materials, and Other Essentials

www.etsy.com

www.frontiercoop.com

www.mountainroseherbs.com

www.specialtybottle.com

Dedication

T his book is dedicated to my dad, who passed just before I landed the deal. It was his greatest wish for me to write and publish a book; wherever he is, I hope he's pleased.

ABOUT THE
Author

W ren Maple, a.k.a. The Thrifty Witch, is the founder of The Thrifty Coven and @TheThriftyWitch on Instagram, a popular and fast-growing resource for witches looking for simple-to-source and easy-to-cast spells. Wren has written about witchcraft and a variety of other topics for pop-culture sites such as Pop Sugar, Teen Vogue, and more. Previous to her witching career, Wren was an editor and writer, contributing to magazines and websites including Martha Stewart, *Better Homes and Gardens*, and other lifestyle publications.

Index